Where It Begins

Also From Helena Hunting

LIES, HEARTS & TRUTHS SERIES
Little Lies
Bitter Sweet Heart
Shattered Truths

ALL IN SERIES
A Lie for a Lie
A Favor for a Favor
A Secret for a Secret
A Kiss for a Kiss

PUCKED SERIES
Pucked (Pucked #1)
Pucked Up (Pucked #2)
Pucked Over (Pucked #3)
Forever Pucked (Pucked #4)
Pucked Under (Pucked #5)
Pucked Off (Pucked #6)
Pucked Love (Pucked #7)
AREA 51: Deleted Scenes & Outtakes
Get Inked
Pucks & Penalties

SHACKING UP SERIES
Shacking Up
Getting Down (Novella)
Hooking Up
I Flipping Love You
Making Up
Handle with Care

SPARK SISTERS SERIES
When Sparks Fly
Starry-Eyed Love
Make A Wish

LAKESIDE SERIES
Love Next Door
Love on the Lake

THE CLIPPED WINGS SERIES
Cupcakes and Ink
Clipped Wings
Between the Cracks
Inked Armor
Cracks in the Armor
Fractures in Ink

STANDALONE NOVELS
The Librarian Principle
Felony Ever After
Before You Ghost (with Debra Anastasia)

FOREVER ROMANCE STANDALONES
The Good Luck Charm
Meet Cute
Kiss my Cupcake
A Love Catastrophe

Where It Begins
A Pucked Novella
By Helena Hunting

1001 DARK NIGHTS
PRESS

Where It Begins
A Pucked Novella
By Helena Hunting

Copyright 2023 Helena Hunting
ISBN: 979-8-88542-049-5

Foreword: Copyright 2014 M. J. Rose

Published by 1001 Dark Nights Press, an imprint of Evil Eye Concepts, Incorporated

All rights reserved. No part of this book may be reproduced, scanned, or distributed in any printed or electronic form without permission. Please do not participate in or encourage piracy of copyrighted materials in violation of the author's rights.

This is a work of fiction. Names, places, characters and incidents are the product of the author's imagination and are fictitious. Any resemblance to actual persons, living or dead, events or establishments is solely coincidental.

Acknowledgments from the Author

Liz and Jillian, thank you for the incredible opportunity to write for 1001 Dark Nights. I had no idea how much fun writing this story was going to be when I first said yes, or how amazing it would be to become part of the 1001 Dark Nights family. This whole process has been such a joy, and revisiting this world and these characters makes my heart so very happy. Huge thank you to the team at 1001 Dark Nights for helping me get this story reader ready and for being such an amazing group of women to work with.

Hubs and Kidlet, you inspire me at every turn. Thank you for being my two favorite people in the whole world and for always being the best cheerleaders. Kidlet, you're the Violet to my Skye. I'm so lucky to have an incredible daughter like you.

Deb, I'm so lucky to have a friend like you and I'm so thrilled that nearly fifteen years of friendship has given us the coolest opportunities.

Sarah, my Hustlers and my SS Crew, thank you for coming on this ridiclously fun ride with me.

Beavers, you're my safe space and my happy place. I hope you love reading about a teenage Violet as much as I loved writing her.

Romance Readers, bloggers, bookstagrammers and booktokkers, thank you for your love of books, and for sharing it with the world. I wouldn't be here without you.

One Thousand and One Dark Nights

Once upon a time, in the future...

I was a student fascinated with stories and learning. I studied philosophy, poetry, history, the occult, and the art and science of love and magic. I had a vast library at my father's home and collected thousands of volumes of fantastic tales.

I learned all about ancient races and bygone times. About myths and legends and dreams of all people through the millennium. And the more I read the stronger my imagination grew until I discovered that I was able to travel into the stories... to actually become part of them.

I wish I could say that I listened to my teacher and respected my gift, as I ought to have. If I had, I would not be telling you this tale now. But I was foolhardy and confused, showing off with bravery.

One afternoon, curious about the myth of the Arabian Nights, I traveled back to ancient Persia to see for myself if it was true that every day Shahryar (Persian: شهريار, "king") married a new virgin, and then sent yesterday's wife to be beheaded. It was written and I had read that by the time he met Scheherazade, the vizier's daughter, he'd killed one thousand women.

Something went wrong with my efforts. I arrived in the midst of the story and somehow exchanged places with Scheherazade — a phenomena that had never occurred before and that still to this day, I cannot explain.

Now I am trapped in that ancient past. I have taken on Scheherazade's life and the only way I can protect myself and stay alive is to do what she did to protect herself and stay alive.

Every night the King calls for me and listens as I spin tales. And when the evening ends and dawn breaks, I stop at a point that leaves him breathless and yearning for more. And so the King spares my life for one more day, so that he might hear the rest of my dark tale.

As soon as I finish a story... I begin a new one... like the one that you, dear reader, have before you now.

Chapter One

Accidental Meeting

Skye

"Vi, if we don't leave in five minutes you'll have to walk to school!" I call down the narrow hallway.

Violet, my teen daughter, steps out of the bathroom with red eyes, shoulders slumped with defeat.

"Baby? What's wrong? Did something happen?"

"I can't get my right contact lens in to save my life." She looks down at the finger crooked in a come-hither motion and squints. "Shitballs, I think I might have dropped it." She flails her free hand in the air. "Great! Just great! Like I'm ever going to find it now."

As a single mom of a teenage girl, I know that one tiny mishap has the potential to ruin an entire day. "Why don't you just wear your glasses? They make your eyes pop."

Violet sigh-groans. "Because I have a Mathletes competition this afternoon, and my plan is to not wear my glasses and also to open the top two buttons on my shirt." She motions to her chest. "So I can throw the other team off with a boob distraction. The combination temporarily fools them into believing I'm unable to math. Also, John Kirkwood always calls me four eyes when I wear my glasses and he's in two of my classes, so I would prefer to avoid the irritation today."

"If he's teasing you, it means he likes you," I point out.

"If we were in middle school, that might ring true, but John is a jerk and a jock. He's a jork. And the only thing he likes about me are these." She pats her right boob.

Violet looks very much like me and not her dad. Which is good because her dad was a one-night stand that turned into the most beautiful surprise I didn't know I needed in my life. Raising Violet on my own hasn't always been easy, but my parents are supportive and I'm lucky to have a stable, well-paying job.

"He's just jealous that you're a smart, independent young woman who's going places."

"It's more likely he's just a jork who makes fun of people because he has a finger penis."

"A finger penis?"

"Yeah." She holds up her index finger. "A penis that's more like a finger. That's the rumor, anyway."

"Men are fragile creatures with easily bruised egos," I muse as I inspect Violet's crooked finger. "Your contact lens is still on your finger. Want me to help you put it in?"

She sighs, but nods. "Can you? I wish I could be successful at putting them in over fifty percent of the time. If I didn't have this Mathlete competition and it wasn't our first time against this team, I would wear the glasses. But the last time we played a new team, I wore contacts and hinted at some cleavage, and two of their team members broke out in hives and another had to breathe into a paper bag."

"Is it fair to use your boobs as a distraction tactic?" I motion her back into the bathroom.

Violet sits on the closed toilet and tips her head back. "Is it fair that girls represent less than ten percent of the Mathletes in our county? Also, I shouldn't have to wear shapeless, burlap-sack style clothes because I'm gifted in the chest department."

I clean her contact lens, tell her to look at the ceiling and pop it in. She blinks a few times and gives me the thumbs up. I'd like to be the mom who says don't use your lady assets for evil, but honestly, she has a point.

Violet has the same math brain I do, and as an accountant working in a firm dominated by men, I can honestly say having boobs is as much of an asset as it is an ass ache.

Violet hugs and thanks me, then rushes to her room to grab her backpack while I return to the kitchen and pour coffee into my travel mug. I pluck my purse from the counter and meet Violet at the front door.

"I'm sorry I can't be there this afternoon," I say as I climb into the SUV.

Violet buckles herself in and tucks her wavy hair behind her ear. "It's not a big deal and listening to people solve math equations isn't exactly riveting for most people."

"Maybe not for everyone, but you know I'd be there if I could."

"I know, mom. It's okay." She pats my arm and smiles. "Mrs. Swanson's recording the whole thing, so we can rewatch and make notes for the next competition."

"Mathletes is far more competitive now than when I was your age."

"Eh, having estrogen on the team is making Mrs. Swanson a little ruthless. There's extra funding available with a set of boobs."

"I'm proud of you for joining," I say and squeeze her arm.

"I needed an extra-curricular, and she was super persistent about it. Also, the potential for a college scholarship is high. I'd like to avoid spending Grandma Hall's inheritance on school if possible."

"We have that education fund set up for you, too," I remind her.

"Yeah, I know, but if I can offset the costs of tuition with a scholarship, I can allocate that money elsewhere."

I smile at my daughter. "You're amazingly responsible, you know that?"

She smiles back at me. "I learned from the best."

I drop Violet at school. "Oh! And don't forget, the team is coming over for pizza and chicken wings after the meet. We want to plan a strategy for our next competition while we're fresh!"

"Right. Yes! Good luck this afternoon!"

"Thanks, mom!" She closes the door and Michael, one of her Mathlete teammates, lopes down the steps to greet her.

With Violet at school, I head downtown, to the office of Freeman Financials. I spend the first two hours of my day in meetings where the higher ups waste my time with nonsense. It's about as exciting as watching paint dry.

I require additional caffeine to make it through the rest of the day, so I stop at the café across the street.

"Skye! How's everything going in the world of numbers on this fine Monday morning?" Larissa, who works behind the counter most days of the week asks.

"Predictable, as numbers usually are. How are you? How are your night classes going?" Larissa is taking evening courses at a local college so she can work full time and earn a degree.

"So far, so good. I'm really enjoying my sociology class. Can I get you the usual?"

"I'll take a twenty-ounce today, and a triple shot of espresso."

Her eyes flare. "Did someone stay up late binge watching their favorite show?"

I chuckle. "I just sat through a meeting that was drier than Saltines in the Sahara and one of my clients handed me all their tax documents yesterday afternoon and they're due tonight, so I have a long day of number crunching ahead."

"Yikes. Sounds like not a lot of fun."

"I'm used to it, and I don't mind working under pressure." I scan the display case and add a pumpkin spice muffin to my order.

"Excellent choice and a perfect pairing for your latte." Larissa hands me the brown bag and I tuck it into my purse.

"Thanks Larissa, have a great rest of your day."

"You too!" She smiles and her attention shifts to the person behind me.

I move aside and wait for my order.

News plays on the TV in the corner with closed captioning scrolling across the screen. It's the usual depressing stuff, so I people watch instead. Several tables hold people reading the paper, other patrons have laptops propped in front of them. Only one pair looks like a potential couple. The local college isn't too far from here and they seem to fit the student profile. The girl ducks her head and blushes, while he picks at the cardboard sleeve around his cup.

I haven't been on a date in ages. Francine in PR wants to set me up with her cousin, but he works in car sales, and I don't really know how much we'd have in common. Besides, Violet is halfway through high school. She needs me now more than ever.

The guy who was behind me takes his place a few feet to the right of me. We make brief eye contact and exchange polite smiles.

He's tall and broad, with dark blond hair, gray flirting at the temples. The crinkles in the corner of his eyes tell me he's probably around forty. He's wearing a crisp navy suit, complemented with a cream button down and a blue and gold striped tie, and brown dress shoes.

Before either of us can make awkward small talk, his phone rings. Fishing it out of his pocket, he checks the screen before he brings the device to his ear. He turns to face the window, giving me his back. He's got a great butt.

I check him out from bottom to top, and when I reach the back of his head, I note he has all his hair. No ice rink for ants forming at his crown yet. Visually, he's what Violet would call a snack.

I smile at the thought and realize he's looking over his shoulder. At me. And I'm appreciating his full head of hair. Yeesh.

I internally wish for my latte to be ready so I can escape my embarrassment.

Hubert, the barista, calls out, "Skye and Sidney! Your lattes are ready!"

I rush forward and grab mine, muttering a hasty, "Thanks!" Then beeline for the exit. Of course, that's the moment a hoard of teens barrel through the door, forcing me to hold it open until the entire gaggle has stormed the café.

Once outside, I hustle to the crosswalk. I punch the button and glare as the sign counts down from thirty.

And then I hear my name being called.

I glance toward the café and, much to my horror, the attractive man whose butt I was admiring is rushing toward me, coffee in hand.

"Hey! You're Skye, right?" he asks.

"Yes. That's me." Maybe he didn't mind my checking out his butt.

"You took the wrong coffee." He taps the side of the cup with the name SKYE written in Larissa's lovely cursive.

"Oh." I turn mine around and see Sidney scrawled on the side. And it's a pumpkin spice latte. Half sweet, skim milk. "Wow. I would have spent the rest of the afternoon working from a bathroom stall if you hadn't caught me." At his questioning expression, I continue with the embarrassing word vomit. "I'm lactose intolerant and this much dairy would mean stomach cramps for days." I bite my lips together and close my eyes. "Sorry. You didn't need to know that. I haven't taken a sip. See. No lipstick prints." I thrust the cup toward him and reluctantly crack a lid.

He's smiling. Widely. "I'm very glad I caught you when I did then. I wouldn't want to be responsible for an afternoon of prolonged discomfort."

We exchange takeout cups. "It would've been my fault for not checking more than the S, but I was trying to escape my embarrassment. Seems like it's following me around and making things worse." I step away from this exceptionally hot man who inspires an unprecedented amount of word vomit. "Thank you for stopping me. You, uh...you didn't drink out of mine, did you?"

"I didn't." His eyes are blue. So vibrant and pretty and his teeth are straight. I glance at his hand. His ring finger is bare. Then I realize he's giving my hand the same inspection. "Do you work around here?"

"Just across the street." I thumb over my shoulder. "You?"

"No, but I'm in the area often." He tucks a hand in his pocket.

"Maybe you'd like to grab a coffee later this week?"

I blink at him. Then open my mouth and ask a stupid question. "Are you asking me out?"

"Unless you're already seeing someone. I didn't see a ring, so I was hopeful." His bottom lip slides through his teeth and for a moment, he looks boyishly handsome.

"But...you don't know anything about me." I don't know why I haven't said yes yet. He's attractive and thoughtful enough to stop me from drinking the wrong coffee. His kindness saved me from ending up curled in the fetal position on a bathroom floor.

He rubs the back of his neck. "I've seen you here before. I've been working up the nerve to introduce myself. Looks like the universe gave me a push in the right direction." He holds up a hand and gives his head a little shake. "I'm probably making this awkward. I'll be here Wednesday at eleven-thirty. Hopefully, I'll see you then." And with that, he turns and disappears into the crowd.

Chapter Two

Tails I Go, Heads I Don't

Skye

"I got asked out on a date," I blurt when Violet walks through the door.

"Cool." She drops her backpack. "The guys are here, too. We're supposed to order pizza and chicken wings, remember?" She thumbs over her shoulder as four gawky teen boys appear behind her.

"Hi boys!" My voice is all pitchy.

"Hi, Miss Hall. Congratulations on the date," Michael, a senior who likely has a crush on my daughter, says.

I'm pretty sure they all have a crush on her, but none of them have enough balls to ask her out. Also, it would make the team dynamic awkward, and Violet isn't interested in any of them. At least not that she's expressed.

"Why don't you guys get comfortable in the living room, and I'll bring sodas in," Violet says.

"I can help with the sodas," Michael offers.

"It's cool. I got it." She plasters on a smile as they file out of the kitchen like awkward baby ducklings. She peeks around the corner before turning back to me. "You forgot they were coming over, huh?"

"I'm sorry. Today was busy. I have a set of taxes to prepare before tomorrow at five, and they're a mess." I motion to the kitchen table, which looks like it was struck by a paper bomb. I have a twenty-four-hour extension, which means tonight will be a long one. "It completely slipped my mind that the boys were coming over."

"It's cool. I'll put out a bowl of chips while we wait." Violet calls the pizza place and orders a lactose free pepperoni pizza for her, a gluten-free barbeque chicken pizza for Michael and Toby, and a meat-lovers for Ali and Kiernan and two orders of wings and chicken fingers. She tells them she has a coupon code for a free extra-large pizza and a pound of wings and once all the discounts are added, she writes the total on the whiteboard.

I pull out my credit card, but she holds up a hand. "The guys have already chipped in. Everyone paid ten bucks."

"They don't need to do that."

"Their moms insisted. It's fine. Now tell me more about this date you got asked on."

I wave a hand around in the air. "I don't know if I'll go."

Violet crosses her arms and props her hip against the counter. "Why not?"

"The timing isn't right."

She pushes her glasses up the bridge of her nose. She must have gotten sick of the contacts at some point today. "I'm almost sixteen, mom. College is just around the corner. I know my plan is to stay local and save on things like rent and unnecessary expenses, and that buys you another three or four years of me living with you, but it would still be good if you started dating."

"So should you," I point out.

"Deflector deflecting." She thumbs over her shoulder, dropping her voice. "Teen boys are more awkward than baby goats and not nearly as cute. I'm in no rush to deal with that nonsense. Besides, thanks to all your pro-self-exploration talks, I have a feeling I'm much better equipped to deal with my own needs than high school boys."

"Amen to that." I raise my hand and Violet slaps it.

"You've dedicated the past decade and a half to making sure I'm a well-rounded young woman. I'm a freaking Mathlete. It's safe to jump back into the dating pool. Unless this guy is creepy. Then take a pass."

"He's not creepy." I fiddle with the charm on my necklace. Violet made it in art class in middle school and I wear it every day. "We can talk about this later. Go hang out with your friends."

"Fine. I'll leave it for now. But we're coming back to this. You're not even forty and I've overheard those guys calling you a MILF more than once." She nods toward the living room.

I make a face. "I did not need to know that."

She kisses me on the cheek. "I'm sorry you can't unknow it, but it's a compliment." She grabs a bag of chips, a bowl, and five sodas before she disappears down the hall to the TV room.

Being a single parent means I have a unique relationship with Violet. We're close, and I don't have many of the issues my colleagues seem to have with their teens.

Sure, she gets cranky when it's shark week, and then complains about the double stomach cramps when she inevitably gives into the craving for a milkshake and compounds her period pains with the moops. We have dairy intolerance in common. But mostly we have a great relationship. She's easygoing and studious. She has nice friends. She doesn't get into trouble.

Maybe she's right. Maybe I should start dating. It's not that I haven't gone out with anyone in the past fifteen years, because I have. But I've been very careful not to mess with what Violet and I have. I would rather be alone than in a relationship with someone who creates tension between me and my daughter. But if the right person came along…well, that would change everything.

* * * *

"You should wear a V-neck instead." Violet rolls off my bed, lands on her ass on the floor with an oof, picks herself off and limp-hops to my closet. "Show off the girls."

"Are we too open with each other?" I run my hands over my hips. I'm wearing black dress pants and a royal blue blouse.

She reappears with a stack of tops. "That depends on who you ask. I also think the more important question is whether it would be better for me to be completely in the dark about how the female body works. Half the girls in my classes are relying on the internet for their information. Which is not the most reliable source. You're my only parent. I'm your only daughter. We're tight. You have rules and I follow most of them most of the time. I'm not an angry teenager who wears all black and acts like spending time with you is akin to going to a funeral. We have fun together. I think it's cool that I get to help you pick out a date appropriate outfit."

"It's just coffee, and I'm still undecided whether I'm going."

"I still can't believe he didn't get your number or give you his." She holds out an embellished top better suited for a night out on the town. "Pair this with a blazer and you're good to go."

If there's one thing Violet is good at, apart from math and spontaneously tripping over air—she gets those two from me—it's putting together outfits.

"And if you were undecided, you wouldn't be putting in this kind of effort."

"Maybe he won't show." I try on the blouse and pull the black blazer over it. She's right. It looks great. But the cleavage is a little much. I add a nude tank with lace trim so the girls aren't the central focus.

"He'll show. He'd be a fool not to." She flops back down on my bed. "This time you need to get a last name, his phone number, and a link to one of his social media accounts. That way we can do some research before date two, *if* you decide you want to see him again."

"Got it, get his last name, phone number and a link to social media."

"Don't get into a car with him."

"We're meeting at a café across from my work."

"Right. Text me when you're back at work, though, okay?"

"I don't have to go, Violet. I can just not show up."

"You need to go. He didn't have to stop you, and he did. He wanted an excuse to talk to you. This is a perfectly safe first date and you deserve more romance in your life than watching the Hallmark channel and *Fifty First Dates*."

"I love that movie."

"I know. Now let's go or I'll be late for first period and then I'll have to walk past John Kirkwood's desk to get to mine and I would prefer if that didn't happen today or any other day."

* * * *

At eleven, I make a trip to the bathroom and freshen up my lipstick. I anxiety pee twice, grab my purse and head across the street to the café. Before I step inside, I text Violet to let her know that I'm going in.

She wishes me luck. And tells me to sneak her a pic, so she knows what he looks like. My palms are sweaty and I'm ridiculously nervous.

It's been a while since I've ventured into the land of dating, and I'm out of practice. The café is busy, but I don't see Sidney anywhere. I check my phone. It's only eleven twenty-two. He said eleven thirty. I order my usual latte and barely resist the cheese croissant. Instead, I get a lavender and lemon scone, which is equally delicious but won't wreak havoc on my intestines.

I sip my latte and try not to obsessively watch the door, but at eleven-thirty-five I get antsy.

Violet messages to ask how it's going.

I hold off on replying in hopes he's running late, but at eleven-forty-one I ask for a to-go bag for my uneaten lavender-lemon scone. The phone rings and Larissa grabs it as she passes me a small bag. "Coffee Emporium, Larissa speaking. How may I help you?"

"Thanks." I turn to leave, the disappointment heavier than I expected.

"Uh yeah, she's right here." Larissa calls out, "Hey Skye, hold on. There's a guy on the phone for you?" Her eyebrow and voice rise with her questioning tone.

I take the phone, my eyebrow arched in return. "Hello?"

"Skye, hey, hi, it's Sidney. I'm so sorry. I witnessed an accident and I'm stuck at the scene."

"Are you okay?" I fiddle with my necklace, my stomach flipping with his anxious tone.

"Yeah. Fine. Rattled, but fine. It seems to be mostly a fender bender. I didn't want you to think I was a no-show. Can I give you my number? Maybe we can try again next week? Or sooner, depending on how you feel about second chances?"

"Um—"

"I promise I'm not in the habit of standing people up. I'd rather be there with you than here."

"Sure, you can give me your number," I concede.

Larissa's eyes light up and she pushes a Sharpie and a piece of paper toward me. Sidney recites his number and I repeat it to him.

"I gotta go. The police finally arrived. I hope I hear from you. Have a good day, Skye." The sirens in the background prove he's telling the truth about the accident.

He ends the call and I pass the phone back to Larissa. "Thanks. Sorry about that. I was supposed to meet someone here, but I didn't have his number," I explain.

Larissa's eyes light up. "Was that the hottie business guy who was in here last week?"

"Yeah, do you know anything about him?"

"He comes in once or twice a week. Always dressed in a suit and super polite."

"That's good. Thanks again, Larissa. I'll see you tomorrow." I leave the café and return to work, not quite so dejected now that I have his number.

Once I'm back in my office, I check my messages. I have two from Violet asking for an update.

> Mom: It didn't work out. I'll fill you in at dinner.

> Violet: 😦

> Mom: It's fine. Have a meeting, chat later. xo

* * * *

"So what the heck happened? Does he dress up as a clown on the weekends or something?" Violet asks as she slices carrots into coins.

I snort. "No. He witnessed a car accident and stuck around so he could give a statement to the police. He called the café, so I'd know he didn't stand me up."

Violet puts her hand to her chest. "Oh, I like him already."

"It was definitely the polite thing to do. And I have his number now." I dredge the chicken through the breading and place the strip on the pan. We're having chicken fingers and fries for dinner, which is a step up from the Pop Tarts Violet suggested. She would eat gummy bears for breakfast if I let her. In her defense, I can't burn those.

Her eyes light up. "Did you get a last name?"

"I didn't. It was a rushed conversation."

"But now you have his number." She pops a carrot coin in her mouth.

"That's right."

She transfers the rest of the carrots into a Corningware pan and drizzles it with olive oil, brown sugar and fresh thyme. "Have you messaged him?"

"Not yet, no."

"Okay, good. I say you wait until tomorrow night to message, just to keep him on his toes. You can open with a question about the accident and if everything worked out. Then let him broach the subject of another date." She sprinkles some salt on the carrots and slides the dish into the oven. "How long should these cook for?"

"You can set the timer for twenty minutes." I finish the chicken and put it beside the carrots. "It's a little hilarious that I'm getting dating advice from my teenage daughter."

"High school is the mecca of dating nonsense. And you can get his last name by telling him you want to add it to his contact, then we can go on a recon mission and find out more stuff about him. Unless his name is something like Smith, then it'll be tougher, but I do love a challenge."

Chapter Three

Take A Chance on Me

Skye

I do not need another coffee, but here I am, entering the café at eleven-thirty-seven the following day. And there he is, sitting at a table by the window with a perfect view of the door and me.

He pushes back his chair, a wry smile gracing his full, luscious lips. I head for him instead of the counter. He tucks a casual hand into his pants pocket. Today he's dressed in a dark gray suit, white button down and a bright blue tie that matches his eyes.

"Let me guess, you were in the area." Obviously, I'm being tongue in cheek.

His gaze moves over me on a slow sweep, and he shakes his head. "I made a detour, hoping I'd run into you. I'm sorry about yesterday. The last thing I wanted was to stand you up, but I couldn't leave the scene without reporting what I witnessed."

"Was everyone okay?"

"Yeah, but a teen rear-ended an elderly lady. I guess he was paying more attention to his cell phone than he was the road. She was pretty shaken up."

"Poor thing. That was good of you to hang around." The flutter in my chest drops to my stomach and then lower, to my excitable parts. Hot men who help little old ladies are apparently a real turn on.

"Just trying to do the right thing, but gotta be honest, it was a tough choice knowing it could mean blowing my shot with you." He runs a hand through his thick hair, his expression chagrined. "And now I'm hoping you might have a little time for that coffee?"

"I can stay for a bit."

Larissa calls my name and holds up a cup, eyebrows rising as her lips tip upward.

"I already took care of it. I figured you'd be in at some point. Guess I just lucked out that you came in today." He motions to the table. "Have a seat. I'll get it for you. Do you want anything else? Something to eat?"

"The coffee is great. Thanks though."

I shrug out of my jacket and take a seat at the small table for two.

Sidney returns a moment later with my coffee and slides into the chair across from me. He really is handsome.

"I'm glad you came in today." He catches his bottom lip between his teeth for a moment.

It's my turn with the slightly embarrassed smile. "If I'm being honest, I only came because you might be here, too."

"Good. That's great. I wasn't sure if I was pushing it since you didn't text."

I sip my coffee and glance out the window. "I planned to do that tonight. After work. I wanted to text last night, but my daughter said I should wait twenty-four hours." I bite my lips together, wishing I could curb my honesty. But I'm not interested in doing the dating dance with a guy who can't handle the complications of being a single parent with a teen.

"How old is your daughter?" he asks, gaze moving over my face as if he's trying to guess my age.

"Fifteen going on twenty-five. She's a Mathlete, very studious and responsible. She's pretty easy as far as teenagers go."

"Fifteen, huh?" He tips his head fractionally.

"I was in my early twenties when I had her." That's as close as I'll get to revealing my age on a first coffee date.

He smiles. "Well, she sounds like a dream. I have a teenage son, too. He's seventeen. He's more of an ongoing concern, but he's always on the ice so he doesn't have much time for trouble."

"Oh? On the ice doing what?" I fight not to fidget. Maybe his son is a figure skater, or a speed skater. But this is Chicago, and people live and breathe hockey around here.

"He plays competitive hockey. We travel a lot for his games. It's just the two of us." I'm not sure what my expression must be, but that smile of his shifts. "Not a fan of hockey?"

"I don't mind the game." I have a love-hate relationship with hockey players, though.

The love part gave me Violet, the hate part revolves around the guy who knocked me up. Violet's father is a former professional hockey player. He was a one-night stand and a poor decision. One I didn't want to involve in our lives after I did the necessary internet research, so I raised Violet on my own. All she knows about him is that he was a fling.

"But..." He fidgets with the napkin, then taps the edge of his paper cup.

I shrug, unwilling to share my most impulsive choices with a guy I've just met, who I may or may not want to see again. "No buts. It must be hard managing that kind of schedule on your own. Are you divorced?" It's always good to know if there's an angry ex involved.

He shakes his head and his gaze shifts to his hands. "Uh, no. Miller's mother passed away when he was three."

My heart clenches. A single dad, with a teen son who plays a high-level sport and he lost his wife. That's a lot of responsibility. And probably baggage. But everyone has baggage. I cover his hand with mine, squeezing gently. "I'm so sorry."

"Me too. She had a rare form of brain cancer. They couldn't operate on the tumor and it just... took over. It was fast moving, so she didn't suffer long." He clears his throat.

"How long were you together?" I withdraw my hand to avoid awkward, prolonged contact.

"Six years. The first five were great, but the last one was hard."

"I can only imagine."

"Anyway." He exhales slowly, his smile sad. "It's been the two of us for a lot of years and he's been pushing the online dating thing, but those apps scare the hell out of me."

"The catfish potential is pretty high these days."

"Yes, this!" He chuckles. "All it takes is one unpleasant experience to taint you for the rest of eternity."

"Mm, so true." I lean back in my chair. "Last year, one of my girlfriends thought it would be fun to set up a profile after we'd been into the margaritas. It was not the best choice."

"Oh, that sounds like it has a story attached to it."

"There were a lot of duck face selfies and regrets involved. I had a lot of interest, though not from guys I would ever want to introduce to my daughter." I wave a hand around in the air. "I shouldn't be telling you this."

"Why not? It's entertaining."

"I'm supposed to put my best foot forward, aren't I? Telling you about my drunk dating app experiences doesn't speak to my good decision making."

"Eh, we all make bad decisions, especially when there are a lot of margaritas involved."

"That's the truth." I clink my paper cup against his then lift it to my lips. "So, what is it exactly that you do for a living?"

"I'm a hockey scout."

I nearly spit spray my coffee in his pretty face. Instead, I suck it back in and cough uncontrollably. The kind of hacking that makes tears spring to my eyes and breathing difficult.

"Are you okay?" Sidney's eyes are wide.

I hold up a hand. "Just." Cough. "Went." Hack. "Down." Wheeze. "The wrong." Cough. "Tube."

He rounds the table and pats me on the back. I raise my hands over my head and the coughing finally stops.

Sidney's hand is still on my back. The warmth seeps into my skin, and I inconveniently consider how it would feel if that hand of his touched me in other exciting places.

But he's a freaking hockey scout. And I've spent the past decade and a half avoiding guys who have anything to do with hockey. Is it entirely rational? Not really. But while my daughter's sperm donor has long since left the league, his brief role in our lives resulted in real trepidation around men affiliated with the sport.

"I need to get back to the office," I blurt.

Sidney frowns. "Oh. Okay. I can walk you out."

"You don't need to do that." I'm already out of my chair, my purse slung over my shoulder, coffee in hand.

"I really don't mind." Sidney follows me to the door and holds it open, then falls into step beside me. "Did I do something wrong?"

"No. I just need to get back to work. I have a meeting this afternoon." At two, so I have oodles of time, but I'm freaking out.

We reach the crosswalk, but before I can press the button Sidney steps in front of me. "What just happened?" His voice is soft, eyes too. "It seemed like things were going well until I told you what I do for a living and now you're bolting."

I'm all discombobulated, and when that happens, sometimes my mouth works independently of my brain. "My daughter's father was a professional hockey player, and she has no idea, and I don't plan to tell her unless it's absolutely necessary because he's a douche canoe and I don't want him in our lives." I slap a hand over my mouth. "Oh my God, if you can just erase those words from your brain that would be great." I glance toward the street. The crosswalk is counting down from twenty. "Thank you for the coffee. You're kind and nice and really, really attractive, but this feels like six degrees of separation and I'm clearly a hot mess. You don't want to date me."

He cocks his head, a wry grin turning up the corner of his mouth. "I don't?"

I shake my head. "I'm a lot to deal with on a good day, and this verbal diarrhea stuff happens more than I'd like." I need to stop talking.

There are ten seconds left on the crosswalk. Nine. Eight…

I bite my lips together and make another terrible decision to distract Sidney and to keep myself from spewing more nonsense. I grab his tie and push up on my toes, mashing my lips against his.

For a moment, he stands there, unmoving and unresponsive. And then his palm settles on my lower back and he pulls me against him, the front of our bodies flush. His hand slides upwards, between my shoulder blades and then under my hair, gently cupping the back of my head as he angles his and parts his lips.

I do the same and his tongue slides against mine.

And I completely forget that this was supposed to be a distraction tactic. I release his tie and run my hand over his firm chest and grip his shoulder. I'm still holding my coffee in the other hand, which isn't the most convenient, but it's half full and dropping it so I can wrap myself fully around this man is both wasteful and littering. So, I keep holding it with one hand and him with the other.

Heat slams through my veins and desire makes everything below the waist tingle. I suck his bottom lip and he makes a low sound in the back of his throat when I follow with teeth.

The sound of horns blaring and someone calling out, "Get a room!" as they pass reminds me we're on the sidewalk, across the street from my work.

I pull away and consider running across the street, but apparently, we've been making out so long the light has changed again.

I open my mouth, but for once, no words come out.

"I disagree." Sidney's eyes are hooded, and his gaze lingers on my lips.

"With what?"

"You said I don't want to date you. And I disagree. I would very much like to see you again."

"Why?"

"Why?" He arches a brow.

"Yes. Why?"

"Because judging from that kiss, we have chemistry. Because you're honest and beautiful and I find you endlessly intriguing. I'm sorry your daughter's father is a douche canoe, and that it's better for you to keep him out of your life, but I'd hate for that one bad experience to be the reason you don't say yes to another date with me." He takes my hand and raises it to his lips. They're soft and warm as they brush across my knuckles, and the contact sends another bolt of lust rocketing through my body. "Have dinner with me on Friday night."

I bite my lip.

"Think about it. You have my number. Text if you want to take a chance on me." He nods toward the crosswalk. "You can escape now. I hope I hear from you."

Chapter Four

The Wait

Sidney

I wanted Skye to say yes right away. I'd hoped she would, especially after she laid that kiss on me. But based on her shocked expression, she hadn't expected the spark that flared between us.

She'd blinked up at me, muttered a thanks and a sorry and rushed across the street, almost tripping on the curb when she stole one last look over her shoulder before she was swallowed by the crowd.

It's been forty-eight hours.

I haven't gone back to the café.

But I have looked up her accounting firm and found her under the list of employees. Skye Hall is a senior accountant at Freeman Financials, and she's been with the firm for nearly fifteen years.

Next, I searched for her on social media. Mostly her feed consists of lactose intolerance memes, a few pictures with her friends during various holidays, a couple of work parties and many pictures of her with her daughter, who looks like a younger, smaller version of her mom.

"Hey dad, you ready to go?" My son, Miller—his hockey friends call him Buck—is standing at the kitchen door, jacket and shoes on, a baseball cap covering his mop of blond hair.

"Yup, ready to roll." I slide my phone in my pocket and grab the keys from the counter, following him outside. "You want to drive to the arena?"

His eyes light up. "Yeah?"

"Yeah, sure, just watch your speed." I toss him the keys and he grins widely, the gap where his front teeth should be a black hole in his otherwise nearly perfect smile.

He lost them when he took a puck to the face last year, which was unfortunate since we were closing in on the end of his battle with braces. He has temporaries for now, but he always takes them out when he's on the ice. Next year, when his jaw stops growing, he'll get implants. He doesn't seem to care much about the missing teeth, and it sure doesn't stop the girls from calling him.

I climb into the passenger seat and Miller gets behind the wheel, still grinning. He buckles up, then checks the mirrors before he punches the directions in the GPS.

"You feeling good about the game on Saturday?" I ask as he pulls out of the driveway.

"Yeah." He grips the wheel at ten and two. "The Cougars haven't been winning much and the last time we played them, we kicked their asses five-one, so we have the advantage. But they got that new kid from out west who shows a lot of promise. I hope it takes him a bit to get comfortable with the team. From what I've seen, he's got speed, but his accuracy isn't the best and I can use that to my advantage."

"Good, good. Sounds like you have a handle on it. We can watch a game and plan strategy tomorrow."

"I have tutoring after school." He drums on the wheel.

"How's that going? How was the English test? You took it in the resource room and they gave you extra time?" Miller was diagnosed with dyslexia as a kid, so reading has always been a challenge, but his school is good about giving him extra time and the assistive devices he needs to be successful.

"Yeah, I took it in the resource room and yeah, I got double time for that. I think it went okay, or as okay as English tests ever go, anyway." He shrugs.

"You want me to pick you up after tutoring and take you to practice?"

"Nah, you don't need to do that. Her house is a couple blocks from the arena, so you can meet me there." He glances at me out of the corner of his eye.

"I thought your tutor was that Anthony kid?"

"Uh yeah, but his schedule and mine didn't work so good, so I got reassigned to this girl named Samantha. She's a senior, and she wants to work with kids who have language exceptionalities or something, so it's a good fit." His cheeks flush and the steering wheel tapping amps up a few notches.

"Is she cute?"

His cheek tics. "I guess. She's nice, and she's patient, and she doesn't mind explaining things more than once. She's got that nerdy library girl look going on."

I make a sound. "Is that your type? The nerdy library girls?"

"Eh, I don't really know if I have a type yet."

"Will her parents be home?"

That flush of his deepens. "Dunno."

My phone buzzes so I slide it out of my pocket and check the message. It's from a number I don't recognize. I key in my passcode and tap on the message.

> I'd like to retract my statement about you not wanting to date me.

> This is Skye btw.

> Skye: We had coffee at The Coffee Emporium, and I stuck my foot in my mouth and then I stuck my tongue in yours.

> Skye: :/

> Skye: Why isn't there an unsend feature on text messages? That needs to be an option.

I laugh and compose a response.

> Sidney: I highly appreciate your lack of filter even in your text messages.

> *Sidney: Especially in your text messages.*

> *Sidney: I hoped I'd hear from you.*

> *Sidney: And I've been replaying the kiss often over the past two days.*

A new message appears:

> *Skye: Good replay or bad replay?*

> *Sidney: Definitely good. Does this mean you're saying yes to the date on Friday?*

> *Skye: Yes. I'm saying yes.*

"Fuck yeah." I fist pump the air.

"What's going on?" Miller glances at me and then refocuses his attention on the road. "Who are you texting? Is it about the draft?"

"Uh no. It's not about the draft. We've got lots of time and there are teams interested in you, so you don't have to worry about that."

"Oh okay. What's got you so excited then? Did someone get signed or something?"

Miller and I don't keep a lot of secrets from each other. Apart from the fact that I'm pretty sure he's hooking up with his current tutor, but he's a seventeen-year-old boy and we've had the safe sex talk. If he wants to do it, he'll find a way. I'd rather it be in a house and bed than the back of a car.

"I have a date."

"Wait, what?" He takes his eyes off the road.

"Stop sign!" I shout.

He hits the brakes, and my phone goes flying. It slams into the dash, hits the passenger door, drops to the floor, and slides under my seat.

"Shit. Sorry. Dammit. Sorry," Miller says. "Are you okay?"

"I'm fine."

The person behind us honks. Miller checks both ways before driving through the intersection, then makes a right into the arena. "A date, huh? You finally give in and message one of those ladies from the app?"

"I met her at a coffee shop."

"Cool." He taps the steering wheel. "When's this date?"

"Friday night. But I can schedule it so we go for dinner after your practice."

"You don't need to do that, Dad. You're always at the arena with me. You can skip a night. And Randy can drive me home. We were talking about seeing that new Marvel movie, anyway."

"You're sure?"

"Positive." He pulls into a spot close to rink three. "That's great that you've got a date, Dad."

* * * *

"Blue or silver tie."

"I say blue. Coordinates with your eyes and the ladies like that." Randy, my son's best friend and teammate, glances over his shoulder before perusing the contents of my fridge. He's a bottomless pit. They both are. "You mind if I heat up this leftover pizza?" He holds up the Ziplock bag containing six slices from last night's dinner.

"Sure, go ahead."

"You gotta split it with me, though. And I agree on the blue tie," Miller's eyes don't lift from the phone in his hand.

"You didn't even look."

"I don't need to. Whenever you wear that tie the moms flirt with you. Wear it on your date."

"Where you going for dinner?" Randy asks.

"Spiaggia."

Randy's eyebrows pop. "Nice, Mr. B. She must be hot."

I chuckle and shake my head. "You boys better get a move on, or you'll be late for practice and then I'll hear it from your coach."

"On it." Miller heads for the front foyer. "Have fun on your date, Dad."

"You still thinking about that movie?" I ask.

"Depends on the timing, but probably. I'll be home around eleven, so I can get a solid seven before the game tomorrow morning."

"Good man. Have a good practice and fun night. Drive safe, Randy."

"You got it, Mr. B. Good luck on your date."

The boys leave and I give myself a final once-over in the hall mirror before I hop into my SUV. Skye said she'd meet me at the restaurant, in lieu of me picking her up.

I arrive fifteen minutes early and take a seat at the bar to wait. I order a scotch on the rocks to help ease the nerves.

Despite the bar being mostly empty, a woman takes the seat beside mine and orders an extra dirty martini. "Hi."

I tip my scotch toward her in acknowledgement. "Good evening."

She gives me an appraising glance. "That it is. I'm celebrating my divorce with a girlfriend tonight. How about you?"

"First date."

Her eyes light up. "Blind date?"

"We've had coffee."

"Hmm." She sips her martini. "Well, if that doesn't work out, you might find me at the bar across the street later." She drags an olive free of the toothpick with her teeth. I think it's supposed to be sexy, but it's just awkward. She puts her hand on my arm and leans in, as if she's planning to tell me a secret.

It's then that I spot Skye at the host stand. She's wearing a curve hugging ice blue dress, and sweet mother of God, the cleavage is damn well drool worthy.

Her gaze shifts my way, then drops to the woman's hand on my arm, before moving to the person attached to it. Her brow arches and I spin on my stool. "If you'll excuse me, my date has arrived." I don't wait for the woman to respond and leave my scotch behind.

My gaze roves over her on a hot sweep as I eat up the distance between us. I take her hand and bring it to my lips. "You look utterly sinful."

"And you look like you want to eat me for dessert." Her gaze darts over my shoulder and she tips her chin up. "Who's your friend?"

"I'm unsure. She's on the prowl. Freshly divorced. It was about to get awkward, so thank you for the save."

Skye's eyebrow lifts. "You're a little too handsome for your own good, aren't you?"

"And you're so beautiful you make it hard to think. This dress is…"

I step back and take her in, working hard not to linger too long on her cleavage. "Stunning."

"My daughter picked it out and called it boobalicious. The poor kid working the host stand couldn't form a complete sentence after I took off my coat, so it's probably a bit much. I apologize in advance if people mistake me for a professional escort. It's the last time I'll take wardrobe advice from my teen." She blows out a breath. "Lord help me. I'm nervous and rambling. This explains my single status for the past decade and a half."

"I think you look fabulous."

"Because of the boobs." She motions to them and rolls her eyes. "Sometimes I wish my mouth would stop running without my permission. I would make out with you again, but it's one thing to do that on a street corner, and totally another in a restaurant. And then people will most definitely assume I'm an escort. Although, maybe not, because you're way too good looking to need to pay for a date."

"Excuse me sir, you left your drink at the bar." The bartender holds out my scotch.

Skye takes the drink from her and tosses it back in one gulp, then covers her mouth with her hand as her eyes water. "Oh, God, that tasted like lighter fluid." She hands the glass back to the bartender. "I don't know what that was, but it wasn't my favorite."

The bartender looks from me to Skye. "It was a seventeen-year-old scotch, ma'am."

"No more scotch for me then."

The host approaches us. "Mr. Butterson, your table is ready."

Skye looks from me to the host and back again. "Is that your actual last name?"

"It is."

"I have never heard that outside of *South Park*."

I laugh and thread my arm through hers, following the host to our table. "It's only slightly better than Ramsbottom."

"I went to high school with a Mike Hunt. Who does that to their kid? And a Richard Dick, which is basically naming your kid Dick Dick."

"Did he own it and go with Dick?"

"No, he tried to go by Rich but he was kind of dorky, so all the jocks who were jerks called him Double Dick. It was awful. The poor guy. I mean, I guess if he was well-endowed it would have been not the worst, but he was the kid who wore the same sweatpants and t-shirt basically every day of the week. I wonder what happened to him. I hope he has a great job and makes lots of money and found his lobster."

We reach our table and I step up to push in Skye's chair before the host can offer. The host disappears as I take the seat across from her. Skye frowns at her cleavage. "This is ridiculous."

I cover my mouth with my hand to hide my smile. "What's ridiculous?"

She motions to her chest. "I don't even have a shawl to hide any of this nonsense."

"I'm partial to the view."

She shakes her head. "I can't believe I let my daughter take control of my wardrobe. I didn't even consider how much worse it would be when I sat down."

"But didn't you sit down on the drive here?"

"Yeah, but I was wearing a jacket, and everything was covered. Anyway, you won't offend me if you have a hard time not looking at them, since they're basically trying to jump out of my bra."

The server greets us and I'm thankful it's a young woman, probably college-aged if I had to guess. I'm over forty and struggling to contain my excitement about the cleavage that is very much on display. I can't imagine a twenty-year-old man-boy would fare much better.

I order another scotch on the rocks, and Skye orders a glass of wine.

"So you work at an accounting firm. How is that?"

"It's very numbery, which I'm a fan of. It's stable and I have benefits which is important as a single parent. The company is good about flexing my hours if Violet has a Mathlete competition, so I can attend most of them."

"I've never experienced a Mathlete competition before. What's that like?"

"Mostly it's a bunch of super nerdy guys who live and breathe numbers. But Violet's math teacher begged her in her freshman year to be on the team. She tried to resist; however, they offer some pretty great perks and scholarships to teams with female members. She decided the potential for social ostracism was worth the possible financial aid in the future. She's nothing if not pragmatic."

"Well, I think it's brave and smart."

"She's definitely both. And clumsy, but that's not her fault. She gets that from me."

The server returns with our drinks and asks if we'd like to order appetizers.

"I'm good with anything apart from dairy. Dairy and I are not friends, and I would prefer not to regret my food choices tomorrow." Skye makes a face like she didn't mean to be that honest.

"Got it, no dairy. How do you feel about calamari?"

"I feel good about it, easy to eat and non-dairy."

"Perfect, we'll have the calamari to start."

The server leaves us to put in the order.

"So…you're a hockey scout. That's kind of a big deal job, isn't it? Always searching for the newest talent." Skye sips her white wine.

"It can be rewarding, especially when I discover a diamond in the rough," I reply.

She smiles. "You love your job, don't you?"

I nod. "Yeah, absolutely."

"Do you play hockey?" She clasps her hand and props her chin on her fingers, effectively cutting off my view of most of her cleavage.

"Recreationally, yeah, and I shoot the puck around with my son. He's a hell of a lot better than I am, so it's not much of a challenge for him, but a damn good workout for me."

Skye's gaze roves over my shoulders and down my arms. "You're definitely in great shape."

"Thanks. Having a teen in competitive sports keeps me active." I tap the edge of my glass. "Tell me about your hobbies. What do you like to do in your spare time?"

She hums. "I'm an avid reader. My daughter enjoys sewing, so we've taken courses together, but I'm not nearly as good at it as she is. I'm not very athletic, I'm afraid. Putting one foot in front of the other without tripping is a win for me most days. I do like to swim, though, since there's a low chance of tripping or pulling a muscle." She reaches for her wineglass but doesn't bring it to her lips. "You're probably looking for someone more athletic, huh? Like a person who wants to hike wilderness trails with you on weekends. I can't even skate." Her throat bobs with a nervous swallow. "I feel like I applied for the wrong job and now my resume is falling short."

"Hey." I cover her hand with mine.

Her gaze lifts, and she bites her lips together.

"I spend an inordinate amount of time in an arena, a boardroom and on the ice. It's my job and I do it for my son because it's his passion. But if I'm completely honest, the last thing I want is to fill my down time with more physical activity. I'm not looking for a gym buddy. I'd rather see a movie, or hang out and talk, or go for a meal, like we are right now." I run my thumb across her knuckles. "I want someone I can have fun with, and if you'd like to learn to skate, I'll gladly teach you."

She laughs. "I'll probably need a helmet and full body pads. I'm not exaggerating when I say I'm uncoordinated. I can and have hurt myself during yoga class."

"That's a lot of bending your body in ways that aren't entirely natural."

"This is true."

The server drops off the calamari and we order our entrees. Skye chooses the steak and twice-baked potato, and I do the same.

Skye delicately lifts one of the calamari rings with her fork and inspects it for a moment. "Sort of looks like a deep-fried cock ring, doesn't it?"

I'm in the middle of a sip of scotch and I choke on the liquid. It burns my throat and lungs as tears spring to my eyes and I cough into my napkin.

Her fork clatters to her plate. "Oh my God, I can't believe those words came out of my mouth. Are you okay?"

I'm still coughing, so she pushes back her chair and comes around to my side of the table, patting me heartily on the back.

"Give me your hands!" She yanks the napkin free and moves to stand beside me. She leans in and takes both of my hands in hers, raising them over my head.

Within a few seconds, my lungs are no longer burning, and the coughing has ceased. I'm also staring directly into Skye's ample cleavage.

"Are you okay?"

"Better than ever," I tell her chest.

She releases my hands, and her finger rests under my chin, tipping my head up. My eyes are slow to follow. Her cheeks are tinged pink, but her smirk is all-knowing.

I clear my throat and settle a hand on her hip and squeeze. "I really love this dress."

The fingers of her free hand skim the back of mine. "Down, boy. We still have to make it through dinner."

I chuckle as she steps back, nearly trips over her own feet, and almost takes out her wine glass. She recovers, though, and settles in her chair without knocking everything to the floor.

"I'm sorry about that. Sometimes words come out of my mouth before I can think them through." She places her napkin in her lap again and picks up her fork, popping the ring into her mouth.

"It wasn't an inaccurate observation." I dip mine in the sauce and chew thoughtfully.

We make it through the rest of dinner without choking or throwing food off the table. It's very clear that Skye and her daughter are extraordinarily close, much like me and Miller. We've also both spent the past decade and a half focused mainly on being a parent and our jobs. She's fun, and quirky and grounded.

And sexy. She's effortlessly attractive, and her dress is literally killing me slowly.

It's only closing in on nine by the time we finish dinner. "What are your plans for the rest of the evening?"

"Violet is practicing at her teammate's house for their upcoming Mathlete competition next week. I'm picking her up around ten-thirty."

"It must be nice to know that she's not out partying."

Skye lifts a shoulder and lets it fall. "She knows teenage boys are all about themselves, and the ones she hangs out with are incredibly awkward and mostly well behaved. Plus, the parents are both structural engineers, and their idea of a fun night is building a Lego city, so…" Her smile is wry. "What about you? What are your plans for the rest of the evening?"

I set my napkin on the table, smoothing it out nervously. "I don't want this date to end yet. My house isn't too far from here if you want to come over for coffee, or tea, or something un-caffeinated."

Skye's bottom lip slides between her teeth.

"But I understand if you're not comfortable with that. We could find a café instead," I add.

"This dress isn't café appropriate," Skye motions to her chest.

I grin. "It might turn some heads."

"I should probably get the girls out of the public eye for a while. They've had enough attention tonight."

"Right. Of course. I completely understand." I swallow the disappointment.

"Do you want to put your address in my GPS in case I lose you on the way back to your place?" She hands me her device.

"Oh." I try to mask my surprise. "Yeah, absolutely." I quickly type my address into her navigation app and when the check arrives, I pass over my credit card, insistent that I pay the tab since I asked her out.

I walk her to her car. "I'll see you in about ten minutes. Drive safe." I hold out my hand and she slips hers into my palm. I kiss her knuckles and she pauses, eyes dipping to my mouth.

She turns and settles her hand on my chest. "Thank you for dinner. It was lovely, apart from when you almost choked to death on your scotch."

"You saved me, though, so thanks for that."

"I've been thinking," she murmurs as she fiddles with the collar of my shirt.

"About?" I hope she hasn't changed her mind about coming to my place.

Her eyes lift. "How much longer I'm going to have to wait to feel your lips on mine again?"

"You don't have to wait, Skye. You can have them whenever you want." I drop my head as she tips hers back. We angle at the same time and her arms wind around my neck while mine circle her waist. We part our lips, tongues sweeping out to tangle with each other. I groan and she sighs as we sink into the kiss.

It's been a damn long time since I've been this attracted to a woman, and my erection is instantaneous and nearly painful. Although, to be fair, the cleavage she's rocking basically gave me a semi for the duration of dinner.

We stand there, making out, until her car dings at her.

"Ugh, stupid car with its stupid annoying alarms," she huffs.

"My house is less than ten minutes away. We can pick up where we left off. No annoying alarms?" I offer.

"Sounds like the best idea ever."

I give her another peck on the lips, then help her into her car and rush over to my SUV. I do my very best not to speed excessively, and also to calm my hard-on, but it's raging now, which, to be honest, isn't a bad thing at my age.

Skye pulls into the driveway a second after me, and we exit our vehicles at the same time. We lace our fingers together as we walk up the front steps. I punch in the door code and usher her inside, locking it behind us. And then our mouths connect once again.

She wrenches her lips from mine long enough to ask, "Will you respect me less if we get naked on the first date?"

"It's technically the second date. Will you respect me less for saying no?"

She tips her head and smiles. "Not even a little."

"Good. Me either."

Our mouths crash together again, and she shoves my suit jacket over my shoulders.

I let my hands roam over all her luscious curves, pausing to squeeze her ass before they drift higher. My lips travel the edge of her jaw and over her collarbones until I reach the soft swell of her right breast. I skim along the bodice of her dress, where the swell dips below the fabric.

She moans softly, and the sound is echoed a moment later. But the pitch is much higher.

One of her hands is in my hair, the other which is currently curved around my belt buckle freezes. "Did you hear that?" she whispers.

I lean back and arch a questioning brow.

Which is the moment another long, loud moan comes from somewhere in the house. Probably the living room.

Skye's nose wrinkles. "Did you leave porn on?"

Chapter Five

Slow it Down

Skye

I don't know why that's where my head jumped to, but the moaning is loud, and high pitched. It's followed by a male grunt and a: "Fuck yeah, just like that."

"Shit. Stay right here, please." Sidney's face contorts into a grimace as he rearranges his hard-on and rushes down the hall.

I could and should stay put, but if he left porn on, the content may make me reconsider another date. So I ignore his request and follow him down the hall, noting how nice his place is. It's a modern build with clean lines and simple decor.

"Randall Ballistic Junior, you cannot have sex on my living room couch!" Sidney bellows as I round the corner.

And wish I didn't.

While the living room is dim, the light from the kitchen shines brightly on the very naked man-boy positioned at the end of the couch, over which an equally naked young woman is bent.

"Shit. Fuck. Sorry Mr. Butterson!" The young man shouts.

Sidney spins around, presumably to avoid another eyeful of naked young woman. He looks absolutely horrified.

"There's a bathroom down the hall to the right. Please tell your friend to put her clothes back on. You can do the same in the kitchen." Sidney says through gritted teeth. His gaze shifts to me. "I'm so sorry."

"There's something in the air tonight, apparently." I fight a giggle.

He bites back a grin.

Our gazes lift to the ceiling when the floor above us creaks.

"Fuck," he mutters. "That's probably my son."

"Why don't you make sure no one tries to jump out the window, and I'll keep these two from attempting a runner before you read them the riot act?" I offer.

"You don't have to do that."

"I don't mind unless you'd rather I go. But you might need someone to drive the girls home? I may be the less awkward option, seeing as I have the same equipment and I'm not the angry dad. Totally up to you, though. And if you want to deal with the upstairs issue before you decide, that's also okay."

"You're amazing." He rushes up the stairs.

I stay where I am, in the middle of the hallway. I'd like to cross my arms, but it makes my ridiculous cleavage more of a problem.

A minute later, the young man whose butt I've seen comes out of the kitchen. He's dressed in a pair of black jeans and a white t-shirt. He's lanky, with dark brown hair that curls around the back of his ears. I note tattoos on his arm as he runs his hand through his hair.

He startles when he sees me, and his gaze darts from my face to my chest and back up. "Oh hey, uh, hi. You must be Sid's date."

"I am."

He nods a bunch of times. "Cool. Uh, I should probably go."

I tip my head. "I'm pretty sure Sidney is planning to tear you a new one for using his house as your sex pad before you do that."

The young woman who was bent over the couch appears in the hallway. She pauses when she sees me, and much like Randall, her gaze drops to my chest before it springs back to my face.

"Um." She appears to be on the verge of tears.

"Is your friend upstairs?" I ask.

She nods once.

"I'm a friend of Miller's dad, and I have a feeling that Randall might need to stick around here for a bit. If you would like, I can drive you and your friend home. Your other option is to be part of the dad wrath. Neither is ideal, but I'm probably the less awkward of your choices."

She bites her lips together. "Do you know where Randy is?"

I tip my head toward the kitchen. "Right here. Would you like a moment?"

"Is that—Can I?"

"Absolutely." I motion for her to go ahead while I move away from the doorway.

They whisper frantically. She's clearly panicking, and as bad as I feel for her, it's also hilarious. A minute later, the pounding of feet on the stairs ends their conversation.

I step out from the hallway just as a young man who is definitely Sidney's son, but with lighter hair, appears at the bottom of the stairs. His face is beet red, and his eyes are wide as saucers. A young woman with sandy brown hair appears behind him, followed by Sidney.

He looks from the group of red-faced teens to me. Apology is written all over his face. And mortification.

"I can take the girls home if you'd like to deal with the boys," I offer.

His son's head whips my way, and his face goes impossibly redder as he mumbles, "Oh my God." He looks like he's trying to sink into the floor. He's a big kid. They're both tall, but where Randall is lanky, Miller is broad, so either of them blending in is impossible.

"I can take Claire and Millie home," Randall all but shouts.

Miller elbows him in the side and Randall grunts.

Sidney crosses his arms. "You two need to explain yourselves."

The girls look at me. I motion them forward.

Sidney's gaze shifts my way. "Are you sure?"

"Absolutely, I'll text when I'm home."

"Thank you. I'm sorry about this." His gaze flicks to the boys.

I smile, irrationally turned on, because managing the boy's behavior is his top priority. "It's okay. We'll talk soon. Girls, let's go."

They scamper down the hall after me. I stoop to pick up Sidney's suit jacket and my coat from the floor. His I hang on the hook; mine I slip through my arms so my boobs are no longer in full force.

The girls shove their feet into their shoes and follow me to my car, whispering to each other. I unlock the doors and they climb into the backseat while I take my place behind the wheel. "Where are we heading?"

"My house." The girl who was upstairs says.

"Are you Millie or Claire?"

"I'm Millie, this is Claire." She thumbs over at Randall's friend.

"Are you going to tell my parents?" Millie asks.

"I wasn't planning to." I set my phone in the holder. "Address please?"

Millie rattles it off and I plug it into the navigation system. It's a twenty-minute drive. Should be lots of time to school these girls.

"How old are you two?" I ask, conversationally.

"Eighteen," they say in unison.

I tap the wheel.

"Are you Buck's dad's girlfriend?" Millie asks.

"We're dating. Casually at this point. Are you Buck's girlfriend?" I fire back. I really don't understand the nickname.

"I...uh. I watch him play a lot. We were supposed to go to the movies tonight, but they were hungry after practice, so we stopped for food, and then we missed the beginning of the movie and decided we could just watch one at Buck's house."

"Which is how you and Miller or Buck, or whatever you want to call him, ended up in his room and you ended up bent over the couch." I thumb over my shoulder at Claire.

"Oh, my God! You had *sex* with Randy?" Millie's voice is about seven octaves too high for the inside of a car.

Claire shrugs. "He's hot. And freaking Jasmine is always bragging about how she hooked up with him last year."

"Okay." I hold up a hand. "As the mother of a teenage girl, I need to step in with some important pearls of wisdom."

"You have a teenage daughter?"

"Yeah, she's fifteen."

"You don't look old enough to have a fifteen-year-old." Claire is obviously trying to suck up.

"That's because I had her when I was young. Her dad was a one-night stand, and we even used a condom. Shit happens."

"Oh snap," Claire says.

"She's a great kid and I'm lucky because it could have been a lot different. Anyway, I'm going to tell you what I've told my daughter. Boys are giant walking hormones. Doesn't matter if they're nice or not, most of their brain activity resides in their pants and they will do and say literally anything to have someone else hold their penis for them. Unless they're super religious and then they find creative ways to make that happen and feel guilty about it afterwards, but I digress. It's normal to want to have sex at your age. But your body needs to be *your* priority." I hold up a finger when Claire opens her mouth to speak. "I'm not done."

She clamps her mouth shut.

"If you cannot give yourself an orgasm, you cannot expect one from someone else. Same sex, opposite sex. I don't care who it is. If you don't know how to get yourself there, you can't ever show someone else how to do it."

"That actually makes sense," Millie says.

"I know. And girls, this is the most important part. Always, *always* make sure you get your orgasm first."

Millie raises her hand like we're in school and I'm not some random mom driving her and her friend home after getting caught doing naughty things with boys.

"But what if—"

"There are no buts, Millie. There are zero buts. Men always reach the big O. Every single damn time. And they get there a hell of a lot faster than we do most of the time. If they can't bother to take care of you before they take care of themselves then they aren't worth your time or energy."

The girls look at each other. "My mom would never talk about this with me," Claire says.

"Well, I'm not your mom, and let me assure you that my daughter usually turns fifty shades of red when I talk about this stuff with her, but you know what she'll never settle for?"

"Not having an orgasm first?"

"Correct. She'll never end up with a guy who won't put in the *effort*. And learning how to push a woman's buttons takes effort and practice and *time*." I'm on a roll now and I can't decide if Violet would be proud of me or if she'd die of embarrassment. Either way, I'll leave a lasting impression on these girls.

"I take a really long time to have an orgasm," Claire admits.

"What's a really long time?"

"I don't know. Like ten minutes maybe?" She wrings her hands.

"Pfft. Ten minutes is *nothing*. Just because a guy can jizz in two minutes, which isn't something to brag about FYI, doesn't mean your ten-minute build up is a long time. Foreplay should take time. Sure, sometimes it's just about the quick and dirty, like when he's looking his best and your whole night has been one giant foreplay session of innocent touches and stolen kisses and him whispering all the naughty things he wants to do to you once you're alone—" I crack a window.

"Oh my God! Oh my God!" Claire shrieks and then slaps a hand over her mouth.

Millie looks at her like she's sprouted a second head. "What the hell is wrong with you?"

"We totally cockblocked you and Buck's dad, didn't we?" Claire looks horrified.

"Yes, honey, you did, but that's not the point I'm trying to make."

Millie wrinkles her nose. "Thinking about parents doing it is weird."

"Mr. Butterson is hot," Claire says.

Millie looks scandalized. "Ew. He's *old*."

"Careful throwing that word around unless you want to walk the rest of the way home," I threaten. I don't mean it, obviously. I wouldn't make teen girls walk home at night in the dark.

"I'm sorry. I don't think you're old," Millie backtracks. "You look like maybe you're thirty, but then that would mean you had your daughter at fourteen and that's really, really young."

"I'm thirty-seven. I had my daughter when I was twenty-one, which is still young to have a kid, especially when the dad ends up being a waste of air." I wave a hand around. "Back to the point, though, ten minutes is not a long time, and you are doing yourself and the guy you're with a huge disservice if you don't help him help you get there. And do not, I repeat, *do not ever* fake an orgasm. No one wins. Especially not you."

The GPS tells me to turn right in half a mile.

"Wait! Go straight! Don't go right." Claire grabs the back of the passenger seat. "I'm not ready to go home yet. Can we take you out for coffee or ice cream or something? There's a really awesome café a couple miles down the road and I have so many questions. Unless you're planning to meet up with Mr. Butterson after you drop us off?"

Claire is way too curious for her own good.

And while the idea of rendezvousing with Sidney is intriguing, it's almost better that this happened. It means prolonging the anticipation. And forcing us to see each other again before we get naked together. Which wouldn't have been entirely gratifying since his son may have come home in the middle. It was a terribly thought-out plan.

"I have to pick my daughter up in an hour. We can hit the café."

Forty minutes and a decaf almond milk latte later, I drop the girls off at Millie's house, armed with all sorts of girl power, and drive to Michael's house. I have messages from Sidney, asking if I made it home more than half an hour ago.

> *Skye: Just dropped them off and I'm picking up my daughter, I'll fill you in once I'm home. Hope the chat with the boys went okay. Dinner was lovely. X*

I message Violet next to let her know I'm in the driveway.

Thirty seconds later she comes tripping down the front steps. She basically throws herself into the passenger seat. Michael is standing at the front window, waving.

"Everything okay?"

"Yup. Everything's fine." Her voice is high and reedy.

"Are you sure?"

"I did something stupid, and we need to leave, so I don't have to keep looking at my mistake. I might have to quit Mathletes."

I back out of the driveway and head for home.

"Can we stop at McDonalds? I need a milkshake and fries," Violet says while wringing her hands.

"Uh oh, you're willing to risk a case of the moops? Whatever happened must have been bad."

"Michael kissed me."

"With or without your permission?"

"With. Sort of. Ugh." She bangs her head against the seat. "So stupid."

"He sort of had your permission? What does that mean?" I point to the glove compartment. "The lactose pills are in there. Take two, so tomorrow isn't another day of mistakes and regrets."

She pops the glove compartment open and rummages around until she finds the bottle, then does some rummaging around in her backpack for her water bottle. She downs two pills, spills water down her chest and huffs dramatically. "Ali, Kiernan and Toby left half an hour ago because Ali finally got his license, and he offered to drive me home too, but Toby ate a pile of raw onions at dinner and I think Kiernan forgot his deodorant this morning and there was no way I was sitting in the car with two stinky boys, plus you were coming to get me and I wanted to hear all about your date, which I still want to hear about. How did that go?"

"Deflector deflecting. Tell me what happened, Violet."

She huffs again and pushes her glasses up her nose. "Michael has a date with Abby Hobbersmith next week and he's had a crush on her for like, forever, and he's never kissed a girl and he was sort of freaking out about it and I don't know what I was thinking, but I told him I could give him some pointers if he wanted them, because I went out with Jordan last year for like, two months, and I got some decent kissing experience from that. But the pointers turned into actual kissing, which surprisingly wasn't terrible. I mean, it's clear he's new at the whole concept, but he's a quick learner and he dialed back on the slobbery tongue real quick." She closes her eyes and shakes her head. "You don't need those details."

"It's fine. You're fifteen. Making out with boys isn't unexpected."

"Anyway, everything was fine, and he was catching on, but his younger sister came downstairs and saw us and then she went and told Michael's mom. She lectured us about not having sex before marriage because she clearly still believes that it's 1950 and now she thinks we're dating!" Violet throws her hands in the air. "And I like Michael, but I don't like, like him. Like, I don't want to be his girlfriend. He's not even remotely my type. I just closed my eyes and pretended he was Tom Welling from *Smallville*. Michael's obsessed with *Star Wars* and he's on my Mathlete team and I can never go to his house again ever. What if he tells the rest of the guys that he kissed me? What the hell am I going to do?"

The Golden Arches appear, and I pull into the drive-thru. There are three cars ahead of us.

"I'm taking it you haven't discussed this with Michael."

"Nope. His sister caught us, ran upstairs, and tattled, and then we got a twenty-minute lecture on inappropriate behavior and then she wanted us to pray for our sins. We kissed! It wasn't like we were humping each other on her rec room furniture! I mean, then maybe we'd deserve the lecture. But our hands were all in PG places and you could have fit an entire extra human between our bodies. The only parts of us that were touching were our lips. And tongues."

Violet stops freaking out while I order her a small vanilla shake and a medium fry. Even with the lactose pills, she'll probably regret this tomorrow, but she's had a hell of a night.

"It was just supposed to be pointers, not a freaking live tutorial. What's wrong with me?"

I pat her hand and wait until I've paid for her snack before I respond. "There's nothing wrong with you, honey. You're a teenage girl and you've been hanging out with these guys for the past two years. That this is the first time you've kissed one of them is pretty amazing, if I'm honest. Every single one of those boys has a crush on you."

"They do not!"

I arch a brow and pull up to the next window.

"If he tells the rest of them, I'll kill him. Oh, shit." She pulls her hood up, and sinks down in her seat.

The window slides open and a gangly teen boy who looks beyond bored asks, "Small vanilla milkshake and a medium fry?"

"That's right."

"Do you want any ketchup packets with that?"

"Violet?" I ask.

"Nope, no ketchup, but thanks," Violet replies, her voice all pitchy.

The boy's head lifts and his eyes light up. "Violet? Hall?"

She drops her hood and adopts a stiff smile. "Hey Jordan, how's it going?"

"Good. I got a part in the play this semester. Are you working on costume design again?"

"Uh, not this time. Mathletes is keeping me on my toes this semester."

"That's too bad. It's nice to see you." He passes over the shake and the bag with the fries. "I threw in some ketchup, anyway. Just in case."

"Thanks. See you around."

"Yeah, have a good night."

I wait until we drive away before I ask. "Would that be the Jordan you got all the practice kissing time in with?"

"Yeah."

"He's cute."

"Yeah."

"Why didn't I ever meet him?"

"Because we only hung out when we were working on the play and he had a kiss scene because he was the lead role. I'm sure you can see where this is going." She pushes her straw into her shake and tries to hide a smirk by taking a hearty slurp. Two seconds later, she's holding the side of her head. "Ahhh, damn, you brain freeze."

"So you practiced that scene together."

"Obviously it was supposed to be closed mouth on stage, but we took creative liberties." She flings a hand around in the air. "Anyway, that happened, and now this has happened, and I don't know how to deal with it. And I'm terrified to text him because his mom probably reads all his messages."

"I read your messages."

"Yeah, but we have an agreement. When it's no longer safe to read my messages, I'll let you know."

"I'm hoping that won't happen for a couple more years."

"Based on what most of the girls I know say about their boyfriends, you don't have much to worry about there. I'd rather wait until the hormones have settled before I go making those kinds of life-altering decisions. My body is mine and all that jazz." She pries the lid off her shake and dips a fry in the thick vanilla. "Ah, fries and ice cream, my arch nemesis and best friend, how I love you so." She hums contentedly as she chews. "Do you want one?"

"I'm okay, but thanks. Back to the Michael issue. I think you can safely message him and ask if he's able to talk. And then you can set the parameters for him. All your concerns are valid, and you can present it to him as valuing his friendship and your working relationship, and that you don't want to disrupt the dynamic on the team, so it would be best if you kept what happened between you," I suggest.

"Okay. I can do that. I'm so glad you're my mom. I can't imagine having to rely on my girlfriends for advice on stuff like this." She pops another fry into her mouth. "Oh! How was the date? Did it go well?"

"It did, actually. We had a lovely dinner at Spiaggia."

"And? Will you see him again?" Violet's hopeful excitement makes me smile.

"I think so, yes."

"Did you get a last name so I can internet stalk him and see what he looks like?"

"I did! His last name is Butterson."

Violet frowns. "Butterson? That's a weird last name. If you marry him, I'm keeping Hall. Violet Butterson doesn't sound as nice as Violet Hall."

I chuckle. "We've been out twice, Vi. Don't get ahead of yourself."

"Still. Doesn't hurt to put that out in the universe." She pulls out her phone, presumably to look him up.

"He has a son," I tell her before she finds out through social media. "He's a little older than you. A junior I think."

Her thumb stills for a moment before continuing to tap along her screen. "Okay. It's b-u-t-t-e-r-s-o-n, right? Spelled like it sounds?"

"Yup, spelled like it sounds."

"Cool. Huh, there are more Buttersons in the world than I realized. The top hit for Sidney Butterson looks like a hockey fan."

"That's him." I grip the wheel nervously. My daughter's approval is important. We've been a pair for a long time, and I don't want to upset the balance. These years before she goes to college and becomes a strong, independent woman are pivotal. I brake at the four-way stop.

"Oh, hey now." She whistles and holds up her phone. "Is this him?"

"Yup, that's Sidney."

"And the beefcake must be his son. He's a junior in high school? He's freaking huge."

"He plays competitive hockey."

"That's unsurprising."

I don't tell Violet about the situation Sidney and I walked in on this evening. I don't want to taint her view of his son before she meets him. And I'm not even sure if that will ever happen. Besides, she's had enough of her own nonsense tonight. She doesn't need more stress on top of the Michael situation.

Chapter Six

You Know Better

Sidney

"Well." I cross my arms. "What do you boys have to say for yourselves?"

"Your date was hot, Mr. B." Randy runs his hand through his hair.

I glare at him.

He drops his gaze to his feet. "Well, she was."

"Shut the F up, dude," Miller mutters.

"I understand that your hormones govern many of your decisions and that it can be a challenge to exercise control over your impulses, but at no point is bending a girl over my couch acceptable. It's damn well disrespectful."

My son's eyes widen, and he glances at his friend.

Randy's cheeks are turning red. "I'm sorry, Mr B. We got carried away."

"Ya think?" I rub the back of my neck. Randy doesn't have it the easiest. His parents are divorced, and his dad is a grade A jackass. Not that I would ever say that to Randy, but his dad isn't much of a role model. "Are you being safe at least?"

"Sir, yes, sir. I always use condoms," Randy says. "I don't want to mess up my future or anyone else's."

I glance at my son. His face is stop sign red. He tucks his hands in his pockets. Then untucks them and clasps them together. "I have condoms too, but I haven't had to use them yet."

Miller is shy compared to Randy, who is proving to be quite the ladies' man. Until last year, Miller had a significant overbite, which we were correcting with braces. And then he got his front teeth knocked out when a puck hit him in the face. For whatever reason, after his front teeth went missing, the girls have been calling a lot more often. It might also have something to do with his massive growth spurt and the thirty pounds of muscles he's put on over the past year.

I point at my son. "Miller, you're grounded for the next two weeks. The only time you're allowed out of the house is for hockey and school."

"But dad—"

"Don't 'but Dad' me. You said you were going to a movie and instead you brought girls home while I was on a damn date. I look like I don't have a handle on what my kid is up to when I'm not around. And maybe I don't." I pace the kitchen. "Randy, you should go home."

"Are you gonna tell my mom?" His eyes are wide with worry.

"What do you think I should do?" I throw it back at him.

He looks from Miller to me and back again. Miller just shrugs, but I can see the same concern echoed in his eyes.

"I don't want to upset her. And I don't want her to think I'll end up being exactly like my dad." He bites his thumbnail.

Most of the time Randy has it together, but his relationship with his parents can be tough. I sigh. "There's a fundraiser coming up and we need help putting together the prizes. You two will spend your time off the ice helping with that. Not as a punishment, but so I know where you are and what you're doing, and so you can give back to the hockey community in a meaningful way that isn't using your promising professional hockey career to get into girls' pants." Randy is a year ahead of Miller and he's already been drafted. As soon as the school year ends, he'll be playing for the farm team in Toronto.

They both nod and mutter their agreement. Randy apologizes, tells Miller he'll see him tomorrow, and leaves.

Miller waits until the front door closes before he speaks. "I'm really sorry, Dad. I didn't mean to mess up your date." He chews on the inside of his lip.

"What were you thinking?" I blow out a breath. "Never mind. I already know the answer. Look son, I understand that you're getting a lot more attention from girls now, and that's only going to increase once you're drafted, but lying about your plans and then bringing girls home is not a good way to show maturity."

"I know, Dad. I'm sorry. It's just...Millie's been coming to a lot of games lately and my room is more private and comfortable than the back seat of Randy's truck."

I choke down a laugh. I honestly don't want to know how often they've used the back of Randy's truck to pull this kind of shit. "What are the most important rules for dating women?"

"Come on, Dad." His cheeks flush and he drops his head.

"Oh, so you can bring girls up to your room and Randy can entertain his in my living room, but you don't want to talk about the important stuff."

He blows out a breath. "No means no."

"That's right. And..." I make a go on motion.

"She can change her mind at any point. Doesn't matter how close I am to getting the puck in the net, if she's not comfortable, then I can get sent back to the bench."

"Correct. What else?" I find using hockey terminology helps make sex talks easier and less awkward.

"Score her goal first before I score one for me." He bites his bottom lip and fights a grin.

I don't even want to know what that's about. I wave him off. "Go to bed. You have a game at eight."

He heads for the stairs. "Dad?"

"Yeah?"

"Sorry I ruined the end of your date."

"You didn't ruin it."

"Well, you brought her back here, and you weren't expecting us to be here, and then she had to drive Millie and Claire home, so we kinda cockblocked you." His eyes go wide. "Shit. That's—sorry, Dad."

"You didn't—" I shake my head. "Go to bed Miller."

"'Kay."

He disappears up the stairs and I head for the fridge and crack a beer, guzzling half of it in three swallows as I cross through to the living room. I pause at the fireplace mantel and pick up the photo of my late wife and our toddler son. I took it before the cancer diagnosis. Before all her hair fell out from the chemo and the weight loss.

Remembering her doesn't hurt as much as it used to. But the hollow pang is still present, still real. Miller doesn't really remember her, which is probably good because the final months were tough. "I'm trying my best. I'm sorry you had to witness that tonight." I scrub a hand over my face, set the photo on the mantel, and flop down on the lounger.

Inviting Skye over was probably premature. Randy's and Miller's antics saved me from moving too fast. We definitely have chemistry, and that dress. Good God, all I wanted to do was peel her out of it. At least I know I can have a three-hour hard-on without the help of chemicals.

I slide my phone out of my pocket and message Skye to see if she got the girls home okay. I need to send her a thank you and apologize. But she doesn't get back to me right away.

I finish my beer, drop it in the recycle bin and go upstairs to get ready for bed. Miller's light is off, so I'm hoping he's asleep. I strip down to my boxers and head for the bathroom. Once I've brushed my teeth, I turn off the lights and climb into bed. It's been more than half an hour since I texted Skye and she still hasn't responded.

I scroll Skye's social media and come across a picture of Skye on vacation with her parents and her daughter. She's wearing a bikini. I'd like to say I keep scrolling, but I don't. Instead, I go to her albums and search for one labeled Beach Vacay.

And I hit the motherlode. There are endless pictures of Skye on the beach, in the restaurant, on excursions, dressed in various outfits. And of course, because she's wearing a bathing suit in many of them, my body starts to react. I consider my options. I can ignore the issue and eventually it will go away, or I can manage it. Option two is far more alluring.

As if she knows what I'm thinking about doing, Skye messages back. I read the message through twice. She's just dropped the girls off. But she left here over an hour ago.

I message back:

> *Sidney: Did you have to drive across town? Is everything okay? Lmk.*

I don't hear back for a while, so I assume she's still driving. I must fall asleep because I'm startled awake by the buzz of my phone on my chest.

> *Skye: Everything's fine on my end. I had a girl-to-girl talk with Claire and Millie and we ended up going to a café that I'm now in love with. Picked up Violet and she had quite the night. Seems like there's something in the air. 12 Hope all went well with the boys. *crossed fingers emoji**

I compose a reply, but it takes a while since my fingers are apparently half asleep, too:

> *Sidney: Talk with the boys was appropriately awkward, but it needed to be had. Thank you for dealing with the girls. That wasn't how I envisioned our date ending. Maybe we can check out that café next week, if you have time in your schedule and I haven't completely scared you off.*

> *Skye: you haven't scared me off at all. The opposite, in fact. I love that your priority was managing your son and his friend tonight, and that you accepted my help with the girls. I would love to see you next week. Let's chat tomorrow and see what works in our schedules.*

"Fuck yeah." I fist pump.

> *Sidney: Miller has a game in the morning, I'll message when he's on the ice. I'm very much looking forward to hearing about your chat with the girls.*

> *Skye: Ha! It was enlightening on both sides. Chat soon. Night.*

> *Sidney: night*

I set my phone on my nightstand and go to sleep with a smile on my face.

Chapter Seven

Can't Get Enough of You

Skye

I check my reflection in the mirror one last time. This evening Sidney and I are going on a dessert date. I decided on jeans and a light sweater. Casual, comfortable. Underneath, I'm wearing a sexy bra and panties. I'm prepared for all possible end of date outcomes.

I find Violet in the living room with a lap pad perched on her thighs and her math textbook beside her. There's a teen drama playing on the TV, the sound so low it's nearly impossible to hear.

"I'll only be gone a couple of hours. Do you need anything before I head out?"

Violet pushes her glasses up her nose. "Nope, I'm good. Just gonna do some practice questions for my finite test next week and watch some hot angsty vampires." She motions to the TV.

I kiss Violet on the cheek. "Text me if you need anything."

"Will do. Have fun on your date."

"Thanks. I'll bring you back a treat from the café."

"Awesome. Thanks."

I leave her to study and drive to the café. Sidney is already there when I arrive, sitting at a table for two. Today he's dressed in jeans and a long-sleeved shirt. A black jacket is slung over the back of his seat and his hair is neatly styled. He looks utterly delicious. His face lights up with a wide smile as his eyes move over me on a slow, appreciative sweep.

When I reach him, he takes my hand and brings it to his lips, kissing my knuckle. That gentle press resonates through my body and settles in my panties.

"Every time I see you, you're more beautiful than the last," he murmurs.

"And every time I see you, I want to get you naked," I blurt, then bite my lips together before I add, "That wasn't what I meant to say."

His grin widens. "I like your honesty, though." He leans in and lowers his voice. "And I also like that we're on the same page. Should we order something so we can attempt to appease the sexual tension with sugar and caffeine?"

"I love that plan, but I also doubt its effectiveness."

"I too, doubt the effectiveness, but I'm willing to give it my most valiant effort." Sidney tips his head toward the counter and his fingertips settle against the dip in my spine.

I don't know what the hell is going on with my body, but even that innocent contact is making me all hot and bothered. I order an almond milk latte and Sidney orders a mocha drink. We move to the dessert case and debate the options, narrow it down to two and we each get a slice to share. I offer to pay this time, and Sidney doesn't fight me, which I appreciate.

Once we have our coffees and desserts, we settle in at the table.

"Can I ask what happened with the girls that you ended up here?" Sidney asks.

I glance around and lean in, lowering my voice. "I gave them the whole, get your O before they get theirs speech and that if a guy isn't willing to take the time to get you there, and you can't tell them what you need to make it happen, then you probably shouldn't be doing what you're doing, and he isn't worth your time."

"That sounds very similar to the talk I had with my son, and like brilliant advice. A lot of the girls that hang out at the arena are pretty starstruck by these boys with promising NHL aspirations. Doesn't matter how much attention he gets, it's on him to make sure he's not the only one getting into the end zone and scoring goals."

"Is it weird that I find your parenting skills sexy?" I ask.

He grins and shakes his head. "Gotta be honest, I was already hopelessly attracted to you, but when you told me you took those girls out for coffee, your appeal skyrocketed into another dimension."

"Remember when we were in our twenties and having a decent job and your own place was good enough to entertain a second date?"

Sidney laughs. "It's amazing how quickly our priorities change."

"Mm. Yes. Definitely. And dating with a teenager is no easy feat."

"It really isn't."

Violet messages to check on me, and I realize it's closing in on ten. Our coffees are long finished, but neither of us touched our desserts, too busy talking. We get takeout boxes and cut our pieces in half so we can experience the best of both worlds and Sidney walks me to my car, which is parked next to his truck.

Sidney sets his dessert on the hood. "Miller has some away games the next couple of weekends and I'm traveling with his team, but maybe we could make another coffee date work during the week?"

"I would love that." I adjust my purse strap and my grip on my own takeout box.

"And I'd love to take you out for dinner again, if you're interested."

"I'm definitely interested."

"Great." His mouth dips to mine and he moves closer. "I'd also love to kiss you goodnight."

"I'm right there with you."

His fingertips drift along the edge of my jaw and then slide into the hair at the nape of my neck. We angle our heads at the same time and our lips connect. I make a soft, needy sound and he groans as our tongues tangle.

I slide my hand up his chest and curve my palm around the back of his neck and find myself pressed against the side of my car. Like the first time we kissed, I'm still holding onto my takeout box, which means I'm limited to single-hand touching. As if he's reading my mind, Sidney's fingers slide down my arm and he takes the box. He must move it to the hood because a second later, his hand settles on my waist, and I have the freedom to touch him with both hands.

So, I do.

And we keep kissing, lips fused, tongues sweeping out to taste each other, lower halves pressed tight. I feel him hard against my stomach. His free hand travels up my side and his thumb rests just under the swell of my breast. I jut my chest out, but we're standing in the middle of a parking lot, so there's not much we can do apart from kiss and make small, desperate noises.

I run my hand down his back and give his ass a squeeze. It's deliciously firm. He grunts and his hand covers my breast.

The thumping bass of a passing car reminds us we're making out in public again.

I break the kiss long enough to ask, "Is your son home?"

Sidney checks his watch. "He'll be home in less than half an hour.

What about your daughter?"

"She is." I glance at his truck. It's one of those nice extended cabs, with a full backseat and tinted windows. The parking lot is quiet, it being a Wednesday at nine-thirty. His son has away games for the next two weekends, and both of our schedules are ridiculously busy. This might be our only chance to get frisky for a while and I'd love to get past first freaking base.

"Wanna make out in the backseat of your truck?" I blurt.

Sidney's brow arches and his gaze moves over my face, as if he's trying to gauge my sincerity. "Yes?"

"Awesome. Me, too." I glance around the parking lot to ensure there are no witnesses. "Let's do it."

Sidney unlocks his truck and holds the door open for me. I climb in and he follows me. I'm right about the spaciousness. The backseat is huge. Three full-grown adults could comfortably sit back here and have leg room. Or two horny parents with teens who make it impossible to get some alone time.

Once the door closes and the interior lights dim, I pull his mouth back to mine. I shift to straddle his lap and shrug out of my coat. Sidney does the same and I slip my hand under his shirt. He's in excellent shape, muscles still defined, likely from practicing with his son.

"Can I touch more of you?" he groans into my mouth.

"That would be amazing," I say breathlessly.

His wide, warm palm slides under my shirt, skimming my side as he makes his way up to my chest. He cups my right breast, his thumb brushing over the bra covered nipple. I moan.

It's been a long time since I've had a man's hands on me, and probably close to two decades since I've made out in the backseat of a vehicle. And back then it was a tiny two door hatchback where even someone as short as me would eat my knees.

Sidney pulls the cup of my bra down to expose my nipple. I arch into the touch as he pushes my shirt up and leans in, covering the tight peak with his mouth. He laves me with his tongue and applies the perfect amount of suction. I slide my hands into his hair and grip the thick strands on a low moan.

One second, I'm straddling his lap and the next I find myself stretched out on the spacious bench seat, my breasts the happy recipient of Sidney's attention.

"You have the most amazing tits," he groans against my skin.

"A good bra is everything."

"You're giving your bra way too much credit." He pushes them together and alternates, sucking one nipple and then the other.

I'm desperate for a little friction, and a lot less clothing in the way. I run my hands down his back and find the hem of his shirt. I tug it up, and Sidney takes the hint and loses it. I hook a leg over his hip and pull him down on top of me. We both sigh in relief when our lower halves connect. I roll my hips and so does he.

"Fuck, Skye, you feel so damn good," he murmurs and then we're back to kissing as we grind on each other.

"So do you," I mumble around his tongue.

We keep up with the dry humping, and the pressure between my thighs continues to build. His hand moves back to my breast and he rolls my nipple between his fingers in time with the shift of his hips.

I'm one of those gloriously fortunate women who can come without a lot of hard work. I don't need all the internal, external direct contact and multiple points of stimulation to get off. I just need the right combination of attraction and friction and I'm good to go. It's a goddamn blessing.

"Don't stop what you're doing." I push down on his ass for a little extra friction. My toes curl as sensation funnels and spirals out, lighting all my nerve endings up like fireworks on the fourth of July. I make random, nonsensical sounds, followed by, "Oh my God, yes." I slap his ass. "Fuck, that's it. My pussy is so damn wet."

My eyes pop open to find Sidney's face hovering above mine, his gaze hot with desire and his lip curled up in a devilish smirk. "Are you coming?"

"What would give you that idea?" I moan-ask.

And suddenly the pressure below my waist is gone. I make a plaintive, annoyed sound and roll my hips against nothing. Sidney shifts so he's kneeling on the floor of the truck and pops the button on my jeans. "Is this okay?" He pauses with his fingers on the zipper.

"I would love it if you would stick your hand down my pants."

He tugs the zipper down and his fingers dip under the waistband of my panties before easing in further. I jolt and moan when he grazes my clit. And then he eases a single finger inside and I experience a full body kegel as the orgasm fires back up all over again.

Sidney curls his finger. "I need to get you naked in a bed."

I attempt to express my agreement, but it dissolves into another moan. Eventually, the orgasm tapers off and I lie there, breathing like I've run a marathon, sated and mostly boneless.

I run my hand down his chest when he comes in for another fervent kiss and cup him through the front of his pants. His eyes flutter closed and his mouth drops open.

"You should sit back so I can take care of you."

I don't have to ask twice. Sidney folds back on his knees and hits his head on the roof of the truck. He adjusts his position and settles on the seat. I unfasten his belt, struggling a little in my zeal to get into his pants. Excitement and nerves fuse as I pull the zipper down. He feels ample through the barrier of his jeans, so I'm crossing my nipples and my vagina lips that his pants package is as delightful as the rest of him.

He's wearing boxer briefs with a hockey pattern on them. I slip my finger under the waistband and hold my breath as I graze the tip with my finger. I glance up for a moment, appreciating the intense, heated expression on Sidney's face, his gaze trained on my hand as I slide it into his boxer briefs and travel the generous length of his erection with my fingertips. His eyes flutter closed and his head falls back against the seat.

"Fuck yes," he groans.

I take a moment to truly appreciate this deliciously hot man, whose ample erection I'm holding in my hand. While he basks in the rapture of having someone else take care of his pleasure needs, I free his cock from his boxers and check out the goods.

"Hell to the yes," I mutter as I take him in.

He has what I would affectionately refer to as a boyfriend dick. Pleasing in both length and girth, with a thick head and a slight curve that will most definitely hit the internal orgasm button when he's thrusting away.

I stroke the length of him, my thumb sweeping over the head before I reverse the circuit.

"Your hands are so fucking soft," he murmurs.

Which is the moment someone knocks on the driver's side window and shines a flashlight into the truck.

Chapter Eight

Shit, Times Ten

Sidney

One second Skye's soft, warm hand is wrapped around my cock and the next she's all the way on the other side of the bench seat. "Oh shit. Is that a *cop*?" She tosses me my shirt. "Oh God. What if we get an indecent exposure charge? What the hell were we thinking? We're acting like teenagers." She rearranges her shirt and buttons up her jeans.

"Roll down your window." The police officer orders while tapping on the glass.

I fish my keys out of my pocket and lean over the center console so I can slide them into the ignition.

"What are you doing?"

"Rolling down the window."

"What are you going to tell him?" Skye's eyes are wide and her fingers are at her lips.

"That we were talking."

"I don't think he'll believe you. You're shirtless and the whole truck smells like my vagina." She cringes. "I wish those words hadn't come out of my mouth."

"Come on, Miller. I know it's you in there. We've had this conversation before and I warned you if it happened again, I'd be talking to your dad about it," the cop says in a bored voice.

Skye and I exchange a look. "Uh oh, looks like we're not the only ones using your backseat for sexy fun times."

Miller will detail my truck as a punishment. After I air it out, of course.

I roll down the window and fight my grimace. I know this cop. And not because my son has apparently been caught more than once making out with a girl in the back seat. His son plays hockey with my son.

His mouth opens and closes and his eyes flare. "Oh hey, Sid."

"Hey Officer Thomas, how's it going?" I prop an arm on the open windowsill, going for casual.

"Oh my God, you know him," Skye mutters from the other side of the truck.

"Well, you just made my night a whole hell of a lot more interesting." He's smirking. He'll definitely give me shit over this at their next practice.

Before I can respond, Skye leans over and blurts, "It was my idea, officer. We both have teenage kids and we're single parents and my daughter's father isn't in the picture, so there aren't any weekends off, not that I mind having my daughter full time. She's amazing and I adore her, but she's a homebody and most of the time her friends come to our place, which again, I don't mind because it means I always know what's going on." She sucks in a breath and motions between us before she continues. "We're trying to date and there is literally no privacy, ever. And the kids are always home, or everything is rushed, or we have to use the back of the truck to make out for twenty minutes so we don't combust from the sexual tension."

Her gaze slides to mine and widens as her hand settles on my arm. "You must be so uncomfortable right now. We really need to find a way to be alone without getting cockblocked or a ticket for indecent exposure." She purses her lips and her attention moves back to Officer Thomas. "I'm so sorry. I babble when I'm nervous and getting caught making out in the parking lot like horny teenagers is pretty high on the mortification scale."

Officer Thomas cough-laughs behind his hand, then slides his thumbs into his belt loops. "I have three teen boys, two are in hockey and one is in robotics. We're chauffeuring those boys around all the time, so I completely understand the challenge of teens. I might suggest a slightly less public spot for saying goodnight in the future, though."

"Yes, officer. Good call. Next time, I won't let my hormones cloud my judgment," Skye says.

He nods to Skye and then turns his attention back to me. "I'll see you at practice tomorrow?"

"Yeah, I'll be there."

He taps the side of the truck. "Have a good night, drive safe."

"Thanks, you too!"

Officer Thomas ambles back to his car and Skye's head drops back against the seat. "I can't believe that just happened. And I can't believe you know him. You sons play hockey together, don't they?"

"They do. Don't worry, though, he won't make a big deal of it." I open the passenger door and climb down, holding out a hand to Skye.

"I'm sorry I left you hanging. I wish I could fix that."

"Don't worry, I can take care of my situation when I get home."

She bites her lip, and her eyes move over me on a hot sweep. "I wish I could be there to help. Next time, I'll take care of you first."

"Next time, hopefully we'll have hours of alone time to take care of each other." I bend and give her a chaste kiss, then hold open the door of her sedan and wait until she's backed out of her spot before I climb back into my truck and head home.

* * * *

The following evening, I'm sitting in the arena, watching my son's practice, when Clyde Thomas drops into the seat beside me. I don't take my eyes off the ice when I say, "Go ahead, get it out of your system so we can move on."

"Hotel rooms have privacy." He props his elbows on his knees and laces his fingers together.

"It was just supposed to be a coffee date, but yeah, we might need to do something like that if we can't find a night when both our kids are out with friends."

He chuckles. "The teen years are tough. They go to bed after you and they're always around. I didn't even know you were dating."

"It's pretty new, but I like her."

"The whole making out in the backseat of your truck gave that away. Where'd you meet her?"

"At a coffee shop. I figured it was better than the apps Miller keeps trying to get me to use." I tap my thigh. "Speaking of my son, what's this about you catching him getting it on with girls in the backseat of my truck?"

Clyde and I know each other enough to make small talk, but getting into my dating situation with him is another level of personal.

"It was a few weeks ago. I caught him with one girl who comes to a lot of the games and practices. They were in the back of the lot."

"Here? At the arena?"

"Yeah." He chuckles.

"It was just that one time?"

"That I caught him? Yeah." He nods once.

I run my hand through my hair. "You'd think with all the energy they're expending on the ice, they wouldn't have any left for things like making out after practice."

"Eh, they're full of hormones."

"Seems like they're not the only ones these days," I mutter.

Chapter Nine

The Moops Ruined It

Skye

Over the next several weeks, Sidney and I go on a handful of dates. Unfortunately, private time is scarce, and our kids thwart every plan to go back to either of our places.

Violet needs to be picked up early from Michael's—that situation seems to have resolved itself now that Michael has a girlfriend—or Miller needs a ride home from his friend's place. If it isn't my daughter, it's his son. On the upside, we've gotten to know each other and outside of the physical attraction, I really like him.

Tonight Violet is going to the movies and sleeping over at her friend's house. Sidney is picking me up in ten minutes. He made dinner reservations and afterward we're making use of my empty house.

Violet is still home when Sidney arrives, but she's in the bathroom. The water isn't running, so I knock on the door. "Honey, I'm on my way out! Have a great night with Sasha and text me if you need anything, okay?"

"Hold on!" A few seconds later she opens the door. She's wearing a bathrobe and her hair is wrapped in a towel. Her glasses fog up as soon as she puts them on. "Oooh, you look pretty. Have fun on your date."

"I will. And you have fun with your friends." I kiss her on the cheek. "I'm only a phone call away."

"Do you have your lactose pills?" she asks.

"Oh crap. Good call. Want to grab me a couple?"

"For sure." A few seconds later she drops two pills into my palm and hands me a glass of water. Her glasses are foggy again.

I down them, thank her and leave her to get ready and meet Sidney at the front door. He's wearing a navy suit with a blue tie that matches my dress.

He taps his bottom lip. "You look fantastic."

"So do you. My daughter's still home, otherwise I would invite you in now."

"She's here?"

"Yeah, her friend is picking her up in an hour. She just got out of the shower."

"Ah, okay. Shall we go, then?"

I grab my purse. "Absolutely." I pull the door closed behind me and make sure it's locked before I lace my arm with his and walk down the driveway to his truck.

Thanks to Violet's smart thinking I don't have to completely avoid dairy. Not that I plan to consume it in copious quantities, just that sometimes they put whipping cream in the soups or to accent desserts and occasionally I enjoy those things.

Dinner is fabulous as usual. Sidney seems to know all the best restaurants in town. I order the butternut squash and pear soup as a starter and the scallops as my entrée, and we finish with the chocolate lava cake for dessert. The conversation is easy as it always seems to be, although our interests vary significantly. And maybe that's why we get along so well. It's easy to keep the conversation flowing when we can share our unique experiences.

Anticipation makes the tension between us flare and Sidney's innocent brushes under the table are making me antsy to get home. I send Violet a text message asking how her night is going and get a quick reply:

> *Violet: At the movies now, don't want to get in trouble for texting, talk ltr.*

I send her a thumbs up and give Sidney a saucy grin. "My house is empty."

He tosses his napkin on the table and signals the server.

Once the bill is paid, we rush to his truck. My stomach tightens in anticipation and I will myself to calm down. But that tightness in my stomach grows as we drive the short distance from the restaurant back to my house.

Sidney sets his hand palm up on the center console and I lace my fingers with his. "I'm excited to see your place."

"I'm excited to get you into my bedroom."

He chuckles. "I'm excited for that, too. It's almost hard to believe it's finally happening."

"I know, right?" An unpleasant gurgle comes from my stomach, so I press my hand against it and feel the unsettling churn under my palm.

"Everything okay?" Sidney asks.

"Oh yeah, fine. Everything's fine." It's probably just nerves and excitement.

But the closer we get to my house, the more noise my stomach makes and then the cramping begins. I can't get my period. Not now. Not tonight.

"You're sure you're okay? You know if you're not ready for me to come over that's okay, Skye. We can take it as slowly as you want."

"I'm really fine. Just nerves and anticipation I think."

Suddenly, I break out in a cold sweat, and the cramps intensify. Thankfully, we're almost at my place. I cross and uncross my legs. Then recross them again.

I don't know what's happening. I took lactose pills before dinner and the chocolate lava cake only had that dollop of whipped cream. I shouldn't have a reaction. When I'm excited or anxious, my reaction is to word vomit and my palms sweat. But this is nothing like that.

As soon as we pull into the driveway, I slam my thumb down on the release and I'm out of the truck before Sidney even has it in park. Another cramp hits as I sprint for the front door, but I'm wearing heels and not tripping over my own feet is a challenge on a good day, let alone when I'm panicking. I'm pretty sure if I don't make it to the bathroom in the next thirty seconds, bad things I won't be able to recover from will happen, and I'll never see Sidney again.

I drop my keys before I can get them into the lock.

Sidney stoops to pick them up before I can. "Take it easy, we have all night, Skye."

I brace a hand on the door. "I really need to get inside." I'm full body sweating now and my stomach cramps again, this time making me double over in pain. This is so bad. So, so bad.

Sidney frowns. "You look like you're not feeling the best."

"It's nerves." My stomach sounds like there's a whole gaggle of angry beasts living inside it.

Sidney slides the key into the lock and it seems to take eleven million years to open the door. I rush down the hall. "Make yourself at home! I'll be down in a couple of minutes." I kick off my heels and take the stairs two at a time, invariably I trip and slide halfway back down, my chin bumping the carpet on the way. I clamber to my feet and make it to the bathroom just in time, slamming the door and turning on the fan, grateful it's old and noisy.

I spend the next several minutes in a death spiral. I'm shaking and sweating and not even a little okay. And then the wave of brutal nausea hits me. It doesn't make sense. Violet gave me two lactose pills and I didn't gorge on cheese or cream. Unless the soup had cream in it. Which is entirely possible. I check the medicine cabinet and realize Violet may have accidentally given me the antacids instead of the lactose pills.

After a while Sidney calls my name.

"I'll be down in a few minutes," I yell. "And please, if you like me at all, do not come up here!"

I hope he heeds my warning and stays where he is. The noise my stomach is making is obscene.

Finally, the worst of it seems to be over. But I'm still shaking and my stomach still sounds like there's a beast living inside it. I'm sweaty and disheveled and I look like a nightmare.

I can't leave him alone in my house forever, and I have no idea how long I've been locked in the bathroom. I spray deodorizer, leave the fan on and close the door, then trudge downstairs to face my date.

He's sitting on the couch in the living room with his phone in his hand. As soon as he sees me, he tosses his device on the cushion beside him and stands. "Are you okay? Do you have food poisoning?" He crosses the room in three long strides and cups my face between his palms. "Babe, I mean this in the nicest possible way, you are always beautiful, but you really don't look so good."

"I think there was dairy in my soup." My stomach yowls angrily.

Sidney's eyebrow shoots up and his gaze darts down.

"I can't really handle dairy. And I thought I took my lactose pills before our date because the last thing I wanted was to end up with gastro distress, but they were right beside the antacids in my cupboard and based on what's happening to my intestines, I believe I took the wrong pills and the next twelve hours will be loud and angry. I basically feel like I have the flu and food poisoning, but I don't have the flu or food poisoning. And sex would be a terrible idea unless you have some strange kinks, and then sex would still be a bad idea, but for very different reasons."

"What can I do to help?" His thumbs brush back and forth along the edge of my jaw, lovely and soothing.

"Nothing really. My body just needs time to stop freaking out and then I'll be fine. In the meantime, it'll sound like there's a battle happening in my stomach and there's also a good chance I'll get the sweats again, which is the opposite of sexy." My word vomit is in full effect. "I'm sorry, Sidney. I was super looking forward to getting you naked and putting some dents in my drywall, but it's not in the cards tonight."

The corner of his mouth quirks up. "Denting the drywall, huh? Sounds like you had quite the night planned."

"I really did. My lingerie game was on point." I sigh. "This sucks so hard. We've been fighting for alone time for weeks and we finally get it and I ruin the night."

"You didn't ruin the night, Skye. I enjoy spending time with you. Do I want to find out if we connect in the bedroom like we do outside of it? Absolutely. But I can be patient." He squeezes my hand. "Now I'm happy to hang out and watch a movie and cuddle on the couch, but I'm not sure if you want me to stick around when you're not feeling great."

I bite my lip, considering. "Maybe an action flick, one with lots of revving engines or fight scenes?" That will at least partially mask the horrifying gurgles from my stomach.

He smiles. "I'm good with action."

I pour him a beer and myself a glass of water, and I take two lactose pills, even though the damage is already done. I'm half-hoping my stomach will settle by the end of the movie, but that doesn't happen.

At midnight we're both falling asleep on the couch, so Sidney kisses me goodnight and heads home. I drag myself up to my bedroom and sigh as I take in my perfectly made, unrumpled bed. I should have had to change the sheets tonight because we made a mess of them, not because I'm a sweaty mess.

At least the worst of it seems to be over.

I change into my pajamas and climb into bed, wishing tonight had gone differently.

Chapter Ten

Let's Try That Again

Skye

I wake up at six twenty-seven the next morning. No matter when I go to bed, I'm up early, even on a Sunday. I use the bathroom, relieved that I no longer look like I'm four months pregnant with a gas baby and that the demons are no longer throwing a concert in my stomach.

I can't believe that happened last night. I also can't believe Sidney stuck around and watched a movie with me. Or that he didn't seem to mind that my stomach was almost as loud as the revving engines and the gunfire.

I flop back down in bed and grab my phone from the nightstand. The last message Violet sent was at eleven-thirty to let me know they were back from the movies. Their plan was to stay up unreasonably late talking about boys, so I wouldn't have to worry about picking her up until sometime around noon. Violet, like most teens, can sleep forever even when she goes to bed at a respectable hour.

Sidney also messaged to let me know he made it home and that he would check on me in the morning.

I slide my feet into my slippers and pad downstairs to the kitchen so I can make myself a pot of coffee and some toast. My stomach feels raw this morning, so simple things like bananas and toast are on the menu.

At seven on the dot my phone buzzes. I key in my passcode and tap it:

> *Sidney: checking to see how you're feeling. I hope your night wasn't too rough after I left.*

I smile. It looks like we're both early risers.

> *Skye: I'm feeling much better, and I slept like the dead. Wreaking havoc on your digestive system does that to a girl. You're up early.*

I've already hit send, otherwise I would edit out the last part, and maybe the sleeping like the dead part, too.

> *Sidney: I'm glad to hear that. I was worried about you. Miller has hockey practice. I just dropped him off. He's grounded from the truck for obvious reasons for the next month. Which means I put myself on chauffeur duty. Not sure who the loser is on this one, tbh.*

I debate my options. Violet won't be home for hours. I feel a million times better than I did last night. We may not get alone time again for a while because Miller has away games coming up and Sidney is traveling with him again.

> *Skye: interested in coffee with me?*

His reply is immediate:

> *Sidney: absolutely, should I come to you?*

> *Skye: that would be great. I just put a pot on.*

> *Sidney: I can be there in twenty*

> Skye: great! See you then

I do a shimmy dance of excitement, and then I get a load of my reflection in the window. "Shit. I need to shower!"

I rush up the stairs, turn the shower on and pull my messy hair up into a ponytail. It doesn't need a wash, but the rest of me sure does. I scrub off the moop sweats in less than five minutes, make sure all my important parts are smooth or groomed and rinse off. I turn off the shower, grab a towel, dry my body, then have to do a second pass because I missed too many areas and trying to moisturize wet skin is a challenge.

I pick my favorite body lotion and rub it all over me, then rush to my dresser and open the bottom drawer, which is where I keep all my sexy things. I'm disappointed that my favorite set isn't wearable because it's dirty, but I pull out the gray and pink lace and satin bra and panty set. It's my second favorite, and it makes my cleavage look fantastic.

I slide into my sexy underthings, but realize I can't execute this plan without changing my sheets first. I've just finished putting on the top sheet when my doorbell rings. I rush to brush my teeth and throw on a robe—getting dressed might be pointless considering I'm prepared for naked sexy fun times. I nearly trip down the stairs and have to calm my breathing so I don't sound like I was running a marathon before I reach the front door. I turn on the hall light and open the door.

Sidney's smile fades as his eyes skim over my grey and pink silk robe. It stops mid-thigh, and much like my bra, does a great job of highlighting my cleavage. It also matches the bra and panty set.

"Hey. Hi. Hello," Sidney says to my chest. "Sorry I'm a little early. It took less time to get here than I thought."

"It's okay." I step back, giving him room to come inside.

"You look like you're feeling better." His gaze moves over me on another heated sweep as he toes off his shoes and shrugs out of his jacket.

"So much better." I hang his coat on an empty hook and motion for him to follow me down the hall to the kitchen. "I don't think I gave you a full tour of the house last night." I try to slide my hands into my pockets, but this robe doesn't have any.

Sidney gives me a lopsided smile. "I didn't make it upstairs."

"I could show you now, if you'd like," I offer. It takes everything in me not to twirl my hair around my finger.

"I would love that."

"Great. Awesome." I lead the way to the stairs and Sidney falls into step behind me. While my robe hits me mid-thigh from the front, I have a booty to compliment my ample boobs, so the back of the robe barely covers my butt cheeks.

Sidney makes a low noise of appreciation and I glance over my shoulder. His eyes are trained on my backside. And because I'm not paying attention to what's in front of me, I trip and miss the next step. Sidney's reaction time is better than mine, and his arm loops around my waist, preventing me from face-planting into the landing.

"Careful now." His lips are at my ear, and I lean against his chest. "No need to rush. I'm not going anywhere anytime soon. Especially not with you looking this edible." He keeps his hand on my hip the rest of the way up and laces our fingers when we reach the top.

"This is my daughter's room." I motion to the closed door with the small empty whiteboard and a door hanger that reads I'M PROBABLY READING. "And that's the bathroom." I fling a hand toward the open door. We decorated it like her name.

When we reach my bedroom, I usher him inside. "And this is where I sleep, and do other things."

"Other things, huh?" He grins.

"Like reading and self-gratification sessions. You know, the usual." I probably should have stopped at reading.

"Your bed looks comfortable." He glances around the space.

I try to see it through his eyes. The comforter is a deep blue, the color scheme mostly cream and navy with a few pops of yellow for color. The bed is half made; the comforter thrown on haphazardly because I ran out of time.

"It is." I cross over and sit on the edge, bouncing twice. I shimmy back a bit and part my legs, patting the space between them. "Wanna test out the springs with me?"

Sidney crosses the room, stopping when his knee touches the inside of mine. "Are you sure you're feeling well enough for that?"

I run my hands up his chest and back down until I reach his belt buckle. "Definitely. How about you?"

"As if no is an option when you're already halfway to getting into my pants." His eyes are hooded as he skims my cheek with gentle fingers.

His nostrils flare when the metal clasp clinks as I unfasten his belt.

I pop the button and drag the zipper down. Today he's wearing a pair of blue hockey print boxers. That seems to be pretty standard for him. I slide my hand inside and wrap my fingers around his erection, freeing him from the fabric.

The last time I had my hands on him, we were in the back seat of his truck and it was dark. I'd felt the length and girth, but seeing it up close and personal...well, that's a whole different bag of gummy bears.

"So pretty," I murmur as I stroke the length and sweep my thumb over the slit when I reach the head.

With Sidney standing between my thighs and me sitting on the low platform bed, all I have to do is lean forward and bend a little to kiss the head. Which is exactly what I do.

"Ah, fuck," Sidney mutters.

I lift my gaze as I stroke up again and smooth my thumb over the spot I just kissed, before dragging my hand back down and pressing my lips to the tip. But instead of pulling away, I part them and cover the crown, circling it with my tongue.

Sidney's fingers slide into my hair, the tips pressing gently against my scalp as he waits to see what I'll do next.

I apply suction, pop off and stroke up again, repeating the same actions, but this time I take him in further.

"Good fucking God, the way you look right now," he makes a deep sound in the back of his throat and the right side of my mouth curls up. He doesn't look like the sweet, polite man who snuggled with me on the couch last night. He looks like he wants to devour me.

I pop off again— "And how do I look?"—before I cover the head once more.

"Like those pretty lips of yours were made to be wrapped around my cock."

I moan at his words and try to smile, but it's tough with a mouth full of cock. I had a feeling he was going to be a lot of fun between the sheets. I keep bobbing, taking as much as I can until the head hits the back of my throat and my eyes threaten to water.

Sidney's fingers tighten in my hair and he guides my mouth, up and down, in and out. His free hand tugs on my robe, pulling it off my shoulder to expose the matching bra.

His eyes slide closed and he groans when the head hits the back of my throat again. As he shifts his hips his eyes open. He tugs my hair, pulling me off his cock. A string of spit connects the tip to my bottom lip.

"Fuck, Skye." He wipes the spit from my chin, gripping it lightly as he tips it up and drops his head, slanting his mouth over mine in a desperate, searing kiss. When he breaks it, his thumb sweeps over my bottom lip, stopping in the center, the pad pressing against my teeth. "As much as I enjoy your mouth, when I come, I want to be inside you."

"I'm a thousand percent on board with that, but I also think you should know for the future that I don't spit." No reason to taste that business twice.

His grin is lascivious. "If I didn't already know you were perfect for me, I sure do now."

I laugh and shimmy back on the bed to make room for him. He climbs up after me, losing his shirt while I lose my robe.

When I reach behind me to undo my bra, Sidney raises a hand. "I would like the honors, if that's okay with you."

"Absolutely." I lay back on the pillows.

Sidney shucks off his pants, grabs his wallet and sets it on the nightstand, then kneels between my thighs. His palms settle on my shins, then slowly smooth upward, over my knees and along my thighs until he reaches my panties. "You are stunning, Skye."

"Thanks, you're firmly entrenched in DILFlandia," I reply.

He smiles, but his gaze drops to where his hands now rest on my waist. My body is far from perfect. I've had a baby, there are stretch marks and I'm hippy, with cellulite and all the other, normal stuff that comes with being a woman in her thirties who has never understood the rules of sports and resorts to yoga and trail walking for exercise. But I love my curves and all my imperfections.

Sidney's hands continue their ascent, stopping to cup my boobs. This bra is good at showing off the girls, and Sidney seems to appreciate them. He spends a couple of minutes nuzzling them, his erection bumping against my pelvis as he makes little noises of appreciation. I reach between us and grip his cock, hoping to refocus his attention on the parts that really matter. He bites the swell of my left breast and groans, but it does the trick. He slides his other hand under me, finds the clasp, and flicks it open. And then my bare breasts are in his hands, and his mouth is covering my right nipple while he thumbs the left.

I stop worrying about getting to the good part, because this man is a magician with his tongue and he looks damn fine with my nipple in his mouth. He moves to the other breast and gives it the same delicious treatment. And then he kisses a path down my stomach. I'm already halfway to an orgasm and anticipation makes everything below the waist clench.

When he hooks his fingers into my panties, I helpfully lift my hips so he can get rid of the pretty, albeit obstructing, fabric. And I part my legs wider to accommodate his broad shoulders. I'm nothing if not a team player, at least with sex. With actual sports, I'm more of a confused spectator.

Sidney is an excellent kisser of face lips, so it's not a surprise to discover that he's also an exceptional kisser of nether lips. He uses exactly the right pressure, alternating between teasing strokes of tongue, soft suction and gentle nibbles. He drives me to the edge of heaven and then pushes me right over into bliss.

Just when I think I can't take any more of the delicious torture, he latches onto my clit and Hoover vacuum sucks it until I'm fisting the sheets and screaming his name loud enough that my elderly neighbors probably have to turn down their hearing aids.

Sidney lifts his head and his lips glisten with girl-gasm. One side of his mouth curves up in a delectable smirk. "Was that okay for you?"

I'm still gripping his hair at the crown, endlessly thankful that he has some to yank on. I tug, not quite gently. "Like you need to ask. Get up here and show me what you can do with that glorious cock of yours."

He prowls up my body, dropping kisses on my stomach and pausing to say hi to my nipple again before he finally kisses my face lips. His hips sink into the cradle of mine and his erection presses against my stomach.

We both do a little bare grinding before he reaches across to the nightstand and grabs his wallet. He rummages around for the condom while still trying to kiss me, but that paired with the grinding is probably too distracting, so eventually he folds back on his knees and extracts the condom.

"How do you want to do this?" I ask as I pluck it from his fingers and tear it open. "Are you in the mood to have me under you so you can pound me into the mattress, or would you prefer to be under me so you can watch the girls dance while I ride you?" I position it at the tip and roll it down the length of him. "I'm thinking we can save doggy-style for another occasion, where we can position ourselves in such a way that we're facing a mirror and we both get a great view of all the fun stuff. And reverse cowgirl is usually best with a mirror, too, otherwise all you're looking at is my ass, and while it's a nice ass, my boobs really steal the show."

"Hmm." Sidney taps his lips, as if he's seriously contemplating his options. "The alpha male in me would love to pound you into the mattress, but the feminist in me wants you to be in control."

"Why don't we start with me on top and we can adjust as required?" I push on his chest and he falls back on his elbows.

"Sounds good to me."

I straddle his hips and grip his cock, rising to run the head over my clit, lining him up with my entrance. And then I sink down, eating up one delightfully thick inch at a time. He groans and I moan and we both sigh when my ass meets his thighs.

His hands rest on my hips and mine are perched on his unreasonably defined abs. "How old are you, anyway?"

"Forty-two, why?"

"You have abs. That seems like something that should disappear when forty hits."

"I spend a lot of time on the ice with my son, and in the gym."

"I drive past three gyms on my way to work every day." I roll my hips and make a happy sound when the head of his cock rubs that elusive spot inside that's hard to reach with anything but a vibrator, long man fingers or an aerodynamically designed penis.

We start moving, me rolling my hips, him holding them to help shift me back and forth, and up and down, both of us making appreciative noises.

"I knew your cock was going to be damn well magical," I moan when it hits the right spot again and sends heat flooding through me.

"Your pussy is tight as a damn fist," Sidney groans.

"Violet was breech. I had a C-section." Not that he needs me to tell him that. I have a scar across my lower belly to prove it. I grab his hands and move them up to my chest. "I need you to hold these so I can bounce without hurting myself."

Sidney happily cups my breasts and I lean into his hands, planting my palms on his chest so I can lift and lower with ease.

"Grab my shoulders," he orders.

I do as he says, and he uses his amazing abs to pull him to a sitting position, so now we're face to face, my chest mashed against his. He cups the back of my head, fingers sliding into my hair and anchoring there so he can angle my head and slide his tongue in my mouth.

We kiss and grind for a minute, the friction on my clit pushing me that much closer to another orgasm. And then I'm lying on the bed again. Sidney stretched out over me, hips rocking into mine, pelvis rubbing on my clit in exactly the right way, the head of his cock stroking me from the inside. He pinches my right nipple, and it's like a direct, psychic link to my already highly sensitive clit. The orgasm hits me with the force of a hurricane and I scream his name and a bunch of other random words, mostly comprising deity praise and accolades to his impressive cock.

I've just regained my vision and the somewhat uncoordinated use of my limbs when Sidney tells me he's going to come. I kegel like it's my damn job and his entire body goes taut, jaw flexed, arms shaking and biceps bulging as he pumps his hips. The headboard thuds against the wall, one, twice, a third time, and I swear I feel his cock bang into my ovaries on his final thrust.

"So fucking good," he grits out.

I have to give it to him. He doesn't collapse on top of me. Sure, he's pressing me into the mattress in the most appealing way. But he's bracing his upper body on his forearms. His forehead rests against the side of my neck. I'm looking down the muscled expanse of his broad back, all the way to the dip in his spine and the ridiculously bubblicious globes of his ass. I run a hand down his back and give the right cheek a light smack. I grin when it jiggles.

He lifts his head and arches a brow.

"Ten out of ten for ass jiggle-ability and pounding me into the mattress."

He smiles.

Which is the moment we hear the pounding of feet on the stairs and my daughter calls out. "Mom? You home? I think the neighbors parked their son's truck in the driveway again!"

Chapter Eleven

I Should Have Known Better

Violet

We've all had a moment where we realize half a second too late that we've walked in on something we can't unknow or unsee. I don't know why I automatically jump to the conclusion that the truck in the driveway belongs to my next-door neighbor's adult son. Maybe because once my mom let him park his truck in our driveway so he wouldn't get a ticket for parking in the overnight lot without a permit? But whatever the reason, I also miss the pair of men's shoes at the front door. Obviously, there's somebody else in this house and it's likely not the next-door neighbor's son. Or if it is the next-door neighbor's son, my mom's MILF status has gone through the roof.

I'm already up the stairs, standing outside my mother's bedroom door. Which is ajar. Not by a couple of inches, either. And in that space is a very bare man-ass and a bunch of intertwined limbs I don't want to examine too closely.

It's when I see the bare ass, that I finally connect the dots. My mom must have texted me seven-hundred and fifty times, give or take 100 either way, asking what time she thought I should pick her up this morning. I kept saying noon on the off chance I'd be able to sleep in at a friend's house, which honestly never happens. And Sasha has a younger brother who is as quiet as a train in the morning, so sleeping in was already a pipe dream.

Logic implies the truck parked in the driveway belongs to the guy my mom has been dating for the last two months. And that means that she, too, had a sleepover. Hers was just a lot more exciting than mine.

"Oh, my God! Why the hell is the goddamn door open?" The question is pointless and redundant. I already know the answer.

My mom did not expect me home at 8:30 in the morning. In fact, she didn't expect to pick me up for at least another 3 1/2 hours and she sure as hell didn't expect me *not* to text before I got a ride home. So, while redundant, the question still feels valid. Because when you have a teenage daughter, learn to expect the unexpected. And that includes my being dropped off several hours early.

"I thought I was picking you up at noon!" mom shouts as I spin around and head for my room.

Half of me wants to walk right back out the front door, but I don't have anywhere to go. There are coffee shops close by, but I'm exhausted from my shitty night's sleep and all I want is a greasy breakfast and a nap. Except now I have man-ass burned behind my eyelids forever.

I close my bedroom door, flop down on the mattress, and pull a pillow over my head. Mom must be serious about this guy if he spent the night. So I probably need to get over seeing his ass.

A few minutes later, footsteps pass my room, one light and one heavier. Clearly the heavier ones belong to The Butt.

Several minutes pass before there's a knock at my door. "Violet, honey, can I come in?"

"As long as no one is naked, sure!"

My door opens and a few seconds later, my mattress dips. "I'm sorry. I thought I was picking you up at noon." She pulls the pillow off my face. She looks as apologetic as I am horrified.

"I should have warned you I was coming home early. I knew you had a date. I should've guessed it would turn into a sleepover, too." Logic and what I just got an eyeful of implies it would have been a safe assumption.

"Sidney didn't sleep over. I ate something with dairy at dinner and I must have taken antacids instead of lactose pills and ended up with demons in my stomach. I invited him for breakfast." She waves a hand around. "Anyway. I thought we had time, but apparently we didn't."

"Wait. I gave you the wrong pills?"

"They were right next to each other in the medicine cabinet. It could have happened to anyone."

"I'm sorry. I feel bad." I frown. "We need a Bat Signal. Like how Toby's older brother always leaves a sock on his doorknob when his girlfriend is over, so Toby doesn't interrupt when they're getting it on."

Toby is one of my Mathlete friends. His brother is a hot jock. He's the quarterback for our high school football team, and he's been dating the head cheerleader since the beginning of the year. They're like a bad nineties' teen movie. They'll probably win prom king and queen at the formal.

"We don't need a Bat signal, it won't happen again."

I frown. "You didn't break up with him, did you?"

"No. I just mean we'll be more careful in the future. And should I be worried about you going over to Toby's place?"

I sit up and cross my legs. "His brother is the one getting busy in his bedroom, not Toby."

"Where are his parents, though?"

"His mom gets home at three fifty-six. She teaches middle school. And his dad works at a bank, I think. Maybe. He always wears a suit. He's home later, but Toby's brother has exactly forty-one minutes to make magic in his room before his mom gets home. And he thinks Toby and all Toby's friends are losers. Literally every time he walks his happy cheerleader girlfriend out before his mom comes home, he makes the L sign on his forehead when he passes us in the living room."

"I don't like Toby's brother."

I shrug. "He's a one-dimensional jork. He's hitting the high point of his life and in ten years he's going to be balding with a beer gut. Based on his last report card, he'll probably get a sports scholarship and have to buy his way through his college courses. He can make fun of us all he wants, but Toby is brilliant and probably going into aerospace. He'll be making minimum a quarter of a million dollars a year for the rest of his life and people will respect his opinion, while his brother's trajectory is a downhill slide after high school. The percentage of jorks who peak in high school is astoundingly high. There must be studies. He can call us losers all he wants, but you can't have brawn without some brains to balance it out."

"God, I love you," Mom says.

I pat her hand. "I know, and I love you, too." I recognize my relationship with my mom is not like most of my friend's relationships with their parents. Is it awkward sometimes? Sure. But life is a lot of awkwardness. If I can't handle awkward with my only parent, then I'm screwed. "Anyway, I appreciate your concern for my mental well-being, but I've been reading raunchy romance novels since I turned thirteen. Would it have been preferable to meet your boyfriend's face before his butt? Sure, but that's not how it went down. Hence, we should figure out a Bat Signal, so our next introduction is a face one." I pull the scrunchie from my hair. "This can be our signal. If there's a scrunchie on the door, then I know there's something going on. And obviously in the future, when I'm planning a sleepover at a friend's, I will now assume you're planning one with Sidney."

Mom purses her lips. "This feels like bad modeling."

"Why? We're just trying to prevent awkward and potentially scarring future scenarios. But if you feel really bad about it, you can always take me to the Waffle House to make up for it." They have the best chocolate chip waffles in the world.

Mom pats my knee. "Come on then."

Chapter Twelve

Let's All Get Along

Skye

Two weeks post our botched date first, Violet-coming-home-during-first-time-sexing, Violet is finally ready to meet Sidney. We decide to keep it brief. He's picking me up for a dinner date. It's the middle of the week and Violet has a physics test tomorrow, so she's spread out over the kitchen table with a bowl of Swedish Fish and her notebook.

She glances up when my heels click on the kitchen floor and whistles. "Looking good. Those jeans are great."

"We're going casual. I can bring you back something from the restaurant."

"Nah. I'll make myself ramen in a bit."

The doorbell rings.

I run my sweaty palms over my hips. "Are you ready to meet him?"

She tips her head. "Are you ready for me to meet him?"

"Yes. I think so. Yes."

"Take a breath, Mom. It'll be fine."

This is the first time I've introduced someone to Violet in over five years. The last guy wasn't bad, but they didn't click the way I'd hoped. And that was the end of him. I really like Sidney. He's stable, a dedicated father, and a lot of fun to be around. And amazing in bed.

"I'll let him in."

"Should I stay here or? —" Violet taps her pencil on the table.

"I'll bring him to you."

"Okay."

I rush down the hall and throw the door open. Sidney's finger is poised over the doorbell. He's wearing a pair of gray casual pants and a golf shirt that hugs his deliciously firm biceps. "Hey. Hi. Sorry to keep you waiting."

His gaze drops to my feet and climbs my body on a slow, heated sweep. "Totally worth it." He wraps his arm around my waist and pulls me in for a kiss. "Hi."

I loop my arms around his neck. "Hi, yourself."

"You look incredible in jeans."

"You look incredible. Full stop."

We grin at each other.

"Ready to go?" he asks, voice low and husky.

"I just need to grab my purse." I swallow down my nerves. "And I thought maybe I could introduce you to Violet."

His smile makes my heart skip a beat. "Yeah. Sure. That'd be great."

"Okay. Great." I nod compulsively and pat his chest. "Just be warned that Violet and I have the same lack of verbal filter."

"Okay." He follows me down the hall.

I clear my throat when I reach the kitchen, which is pointless because my heels announce me, anyway.

Violet is sitting at the kitchen table with her pencil poised between her fingers, her eyes on the doorway we're now occupying.

"Violet, honey, I'd like you to meet Sidney. Sidney, this is my daughter, Violet," I sweep out a hand like I've suddenly turned into Vanna White, but younger and with darker hair, and a lot shorter, with no sparkly dress.

He steps into the kitchen as Violet pushes her chair back. Unfortunately, neither of us is known for our stellar coordination, so her chair goes clattering to the floor and Violet goes down with it.

Sidney rushes around the table and helps her to her feet. I nab her glasses from the floor and pass them back to her.

"Are you okay?" Sidney asks.

"I'm fine. Embarrassed, but fine." Violet's neck turns red in patches. She holds out her hand. "Hi, it's nice to meet your face in three-dimensions instead of your butt." She slaps her hand over her eyes. "Oh my God. Please don't break up with my mom because my mouth is stupid."

Sidney chuckles. "I'm sorry our first introduction left such an unfortunate and lasting impression."

Violet drops her hand. "It could've been worse. I could've seen your dangler and not your butt." Her eyes bug out. "I'm sorry, Mom. So sorry. I'd like to say I'm not always like this, but that would be a lie. It calms down a little with subsequent interactions, though. People make me nervous, especially new people, and you're a new people. Instead of losing my ability to speak, I word vomit the first thing that pops into my head. Maybe by interaction three or four I'll just say normal things. It's nice to meet you. Again, please don't break up with my mom. She really likes you and this is the first time I've seen her this happy in like...I don't know. I'm going to stop talking now." She bites her lips together and her eyes dart briefly to me.

Thankfully, Sidney has spent enough time with me that Violet's rant seems normal. "I'm glad to hear that your mom likes me and that I make her happy."

"She had stars in her eyes for days after that morning delight," Violet says, then gives me an imploring look. "You two should go. I'm at maximum capacity for embarrassment tolerance and I don't think my word hole is going to stop with the truth vomit anytime soon."

I skirt around Sidney and hug my daughter.

"I'm so sorry, Mom."

I pat her back. "You did great."

"Liar face." She kisses my cheek. "Have fun, though."

"Take an antihistamine, but not the non-drowsy ones, otherwise you'll be up all night."

"Good call. I can feel the hives setting in."

She nods and waves when Sidney says it was nice to meet her. I usher him out the door.

"That went well," I say once we're safely inside his truck.

"You think so?" Sidney taps on the steering wheel.

"Oh yeah, definitely. A couple more brief hellos and the word vomit will slow to a trickle. She just needs time to get comfortable." And get over the fact that she's seen his bare butt. "Exposure therapy is the best way to get over the nerves."

"I can handle more exposure therapy. Once she gets comfortable enough with me, maybe we can try getting the kids together. Eventually. No rush, though. I know that's kind a big step." More steering wheel tapping.

I shift in my seat so I can stare at his profile. "You like me that much, huh?"

He glances at me out of the corner of his eye. "Is that a serious question?"

I open and close my mouth a couple of times. "I mean…even talking about getting the kids together sort of implies a level of seriousness."

"I feel pretty serious about you," he says softly.

"I feel the same. I was nervous about you meeting Vi because I really want her to like you," I admit.

"And you think she does?" he asks.

"Yeah, definitely. She would have texted me already if you'd gotten a thumbs down," I assure him.

We arrive at the restaurant, and he backs the truck into a spot. He shifts into park, but his hands stay on the wheel, gripping tightly.

"Is everything okay, Sid?"

"Yeah. Everything's great." He releases the steering wheel and turns off the engine.

I follow his lead and get out of the truck.

The place we're going tonight is causal, but it has the prettiest rose and ivy covered gazebo. He laces his fingers with mine and heads in that direction instead of the entrance to the restaurant. When we're standing in the middle he stops and takes my other hand. He looks down at our clasped hands.

I give his a squeeze. "Are you sure everything is okay?"

"Positive." He blows out a breath and his gaze lifts to mine. "I don't think I recognized how nervous I was about meeting Violet until a minute ago."

"She likes you, you have nothing to worry about."

"That's good." He smiles and brings my hands to his lips kissing my knuckles. "Because I just realized I'm totally in love with you."

I blink at him a few times. I know how I feel about him, but hearing him say it first is kind of a shock. "Are you sure?"

He bites his lips together and nods once. "It's okay if you're not there yet."

"I'm there. I'm here. With you. In the love boat. Or gazebo." I fling a hand around. "I just didn't expect you to say it first. But I've been thinking it a lot lately. In my head, obviously."

His uncertain expression shifts to amusement. "Have you?"

"Often right after sex and especially after you've gone down on me, but also when you text me in the morning, and at night, or flowers show up at my work, or whenever I see you, to be perfectly honest." I link my hands behind his neck. "It's been a struggle keeping it to myself lately, so I'm glad you had the bigger balls of the two of us and made it easy for me to admit I feel the same way." I'm rambling, which isn't unusual during a bout of nerves. "This is a really perfect spot for an ILY drop."

"I agree."

"I love you, too," I whisper. "Now you should kiss me."

He dips down and brushes his lips over mine and my happy heart melts while my toes curl. Today couldn't be more perfect.

* * * *

Despite the ILY drop, we don't get the kids together right away. I'm just happy to feel all the feelings without adding the anxiety of hoping our kids get along, so we've been dating several months when Sidney proposes a backyard barbeque at his place, so Vi and Miller can meet. This is the big test.

Miller is a nice kid. School isn't his favorite, but he's dedicated to hockey. A bit of a follower with his friends, but his best buddy just got picked up by Toronto and has moved out there for training camp, so Miller's been focused on hockey these days, according to Sidney. Now that he has a friend in the pros, he's doubling his efforts on the ice so he can join him next year.

Violet and I load our beach bags into the car—Sidney has a swimming pool—and drive across town.

Exposure therapy with Violet worked well with Sidney, and as predicted, the word vomit shifted into normal conversation after the first few meetings. Or as normal as conversation gets with Violet, anyway.

"Wow, this is a swanky neighborhood. Hockey scouts must do pretty well, huh?" Violet pushes her glasses up her nose.

"Seems that way." We haven't talked about finances, but based on his house, his car and the way he dresses, scouts do okay.

I pull into Sidney's driveway. I've been to his place a few times now. Since his son often has long hockey practices in the evening, sometimes we order takeout instead of going to a restaurant so we can get in some sexy time without worrying about anyone's ass being on display in front of our teenagers.

"Our house looks like something this house birthed," Violet observes.

"It's significantly bigger," I agree.

I do just fine on my own, but not hockey scout fine. Violet and I live in a small two-bedroom townhouse with a backyard the size of a postage stamp. But it's ours and we've made it home.

Sidney has no chill. We're not even out of the car and he's already rushing down the front steps to greet us. "Hi Violet, hi Skye. Can I help bring anything in?"

"I have a meat and cheese tray in the trunk and dessert."

"You didn't need to bring anything but your beautiful self and a bathing suit." He kisses me on the cheek. "I hope you brought your suit, too." He smiles at Violet.

She pushes her glasses up her nose. "I did. You have a lovely house. From the outside. I'm guessing the inside will be the same because it wouldn't make much sense to have a house this nice with insides that resemble a meth lab."

Sidney chuckles. "It's a bit of a man cave."

"Makes sense since you're a man." Violet shoulders her bag and grabs mine too so I can bring in the cheese tray and Sidney can bring in the dessert.

"These look amazing. What's the dessert?"

"It's a lactose-free, red velvet cake."

I ordered the cheese tray and dessert from a small independently run caterer who lets me bring in my own serving dishes. It makes me look like I put in the effort. She also carries a wide variety of lactose-free cheeses so Violet and I can indulge without living in the bathroom for the next three days. I'm not the best cook in the world, but Violet and I get by. Salad is a big winner in the summer in our house because it's hard to screw up.

Sidney ushers us inside. "Don't bother taking off your shoes. We'll head to the backyard. Miller's already out there." He sets the dessert on the counter. "All his friends call him Buck, though, so he might want you to call him that instead, Violet."

"Is it his middle name?" Violet asks.

"No, just a nickname he picked up in hockey and it seems to have stuck." He puts the beer in the fridge and takes the cheese tray from me. "This is the kitchen, and there's a powder room down the hall. We have a pool house out back where you can change into your suit when you're ready," he tells Violet.

He motions for us to follow him, his smile wide, if not a little nervous.

"This house is really, really nice, Mom," Violet whispers.

"It is," I agree.

The living room boasts a dark leather couch and two club chairs.

One wall contains framed pictures of Sidney with various hockey players, possibly all the ones he's scouted throughout his career. Most of them seem to be signed by the players. A huge flatscreen TV takes up the wall across from the couch, and under that is a gas burning fireplace. The whole room screams man-sporty.

Violet nearly trips on her way outside, but I grab her arm to keep her from going down.

Siphoning leaves out of the pool with a net is Miller.

He's dressed in a t-shirt with a hockey logo, board shorts and a baseball cap. He looks like any teenage boy, except broader. The kid is nearly as thick as his dad and he's only seventeen.

Sidney and I exchange nervous smiles. It doesn't matter how into each other we are, we can't take it to the next level if our kids don't mesh.

Chapter Thirteen

Stepsister Potential

Miller

I glance up at the sound of the screen door sliding closed. This is it. The big introduction. I'm about to meet my dad's girlfriend's teenage daughter. This could go one of two ways; good or not good.

The first thing I notice about Skye and Violet is that they're basically carbon copies of each other. Except Violet is a little shorter than her mom. And obviously younger. They have the same long, dark, wavy hair. The same body type. The same mannerisms, even.

I set the net in the holder and wipe my hands on my shorts. Dad smiles as I approach, but he's doing that thing where he taps on his leg, a sure sign he's nervous. That makes two of us.

"Hi Skye, you look nice today," I say.

"Hi Miller, thank you." Skye looks just as nervous as my dad, and her eyes keep darting to her daughter. "Miller, this is my daughter, Violet. Violet, this is Miller, Sidney's son. He's in high school, too."

Violet lifts her hand in an awkward wave, then pushes her glasses up her nose. "Hi. It's nice to meet you."

I wave back. "Yeah. You, too." I wish my best friend wasn't already in training camp this summer. He's ultra-smooth with the ladies where I'm not. Not that I need to be smooth with my maybe-future-stepsister, but not awkward would be a good start.

"Miller, why don't you take Violet to the pool house so she can change into her bathing suit, and you can grab her a soda while you're at it?" Dad turns to Skye. "You can get changed in the house and we can bring out that delicious-looking cheese tray."

Skye beams at my dad. "That sounds great. Violet, is that okay with you?"

Violet shrugs. "Sure."

My dad and Skye disappear inside, leaving me alone with Violet.

"Whelp, this is nice and awkward, isn't it?"

I grin. "Yeah. Kinda. Want me to show you the pool house?"

"Might as well, since I'm pretty sure our parents are about to get their bone on."

I glance toward the house. "Seriously?"

"Based on the way they were eyeing each other, yeah." Her slides slap the deck. "Let's move away from the house so we don't hear anything that will result in us needing therapy to recover from."

I follow her across the patio to the pool house. "You're tiny," I observe.

"Or maybe you're just unusually large. How old are you?"

"Seventeen."

"How tall are you?"

"Six-two and a half."

Violet snorts. "Like you need to add the extra half inch when you're already over six feet. I'm barely five-four. I need every single one of those inches to count, partial or not."

"Bet you can fit in any backseat without a problem."

"True, but I always end up in the middle seat and that sucks the D. Especially in those really old cars with the hump on the floor."

I rush to get in front of her when we reach the pool house so I can be polite and open the door for her. "That's legit."

She steps over the threshold and whistles. "You have a TV in your pool house?"

"Yeah. This is where me and my buddies hang out. There's a bedroom through there if you want to change." I point across the room.

"Sure. Thanks."

I rummage around in the fridge and line up a selection of sodas on the counter while I wait. A few minutes later, she returns wearing a beach cover up and she's piled her hair on top of her head in a huge, puffy bun.

"Want something to drink?" I motion to the counter.

"Ooooh, I haven't had grape soda since I was a kid. I'll take one of those."

"Cool." I hand her the can and take an orange soda for myself. "We can spike them."

Violet arches a brow. "Tempting, but I'm a lightweight and awkward with the word vomit when I'm sober. Pretty sure I don't want to add booze to the mix."

"Fair." I gulp down some soda and replace it with the contents of a tiny vodka bottle, hiding it under an empty bag of Doritos in the garbage before we head outside.

Violet takes a lounge chair in the shade. I strip off my shirt and take the lounger beside her. Nothing is worse than a t-shirt tan.

"You're fuzzy as fuck." Violet gently pats my arm hair, then snatches her hand away. "Shit. Sorry. That was weird. And awkward. You have a lot of chest hair for a teenager. I mean, it's blond, so like, mostly blends in, but it's almost like an optical illusion. You have a blond aura of protection. Imagine if that was an actual superpower? Like your body fuzz was a magic repelling force field!"

I stare at her, waiting to see what else will come out of her mouth.

"Sorry. I suffer from word vomit. It's worse when I'm nervous, but it never really goes away."

"My dad sort of warned me about that," I admit.

"That was smart of him. Seriously, you must be the envy of all the dude-bros in your grade," Violet says.

I run my hand over my chest. "I'm due for a trim."

"A trim?"

"Yeah. I use a number four trimmer in the summer. Keeps the mosquitoes from getting caught in my arm hair."

"That makes sense. It would be a good insulator in the winter, though." She grins. "You're like a yeti."

I snort-laugh. I could get used to Violet.

"So let's talk about our 'rents before they come out. If we're meeting, that means they must be pretty serious, right?"

I nod. "Seems that way."

"I haven't met one of my mom's boyfriends since middle school. How about you?"

"There was one woman in my freshman year. She had two younger kids, I think, but I never met them, and they only dated for like, a couple of months, maybe?"

"And our parents have been dating for what, like, five months now?"

"That sounds about right." I sip my drink. "My dad's been working out with me a lot more lately, maybe trying to buff up for the summer."

"Or he's trying to buff up for all the boning they're doing," Violet mutters. "He's got an ass you can bounce a quarter off of, that's for sure."

I spit spray my drink all over my chest. "You checked out my dad's ass?"

"Not on purpose." Violet makes a face. "The first time I met him they were doing the horizontal tango."

"Wait. What?"

Violet waves a hand around and almost smacks herself in the face. "Nothing. Never mind. It's not important."

"You can't say something like that and then wave it off."

She sighs, but launches into the story. Her face grows progressively redder and by the time she gets to the part about my dad's bare ass, she looks like she might burst into flames.

"Wow."

"Yeah."

I don't share the story about getting caught bringing girls home by my dad and Skye. Or that Skye drove the girls home and apparently took them out for coffee and dessert afterward.

Dad and Skye return, both wearing huge grins. We eat snacks and talk. I find out Violet is a math nerd, and she gets all A's in school. I'm more of a C-minus student. Especially with English, since I'm dyslexic. But I have a tutor for that. Although, if I'm honest, we don't spend a lot of time on the tutoring part. I've gotten really good at giving orgasms, and not all that good at writing essays.

It gets hot in the afternoon, so we jump in the pool. Violet falls in no less than three times over the course of the afternoon. Dad barbeques steak, corn and salad for dinner and Violet and I offer to take care of dishes, mostly because our parents are making eyes at each other and it's gross.

"Okay, so I'm all about probability and statistics, and taking into account past relationships and present circumstances…" Violet says as she scrapes the plates into the garbage disposal.

"Math isn't my favorite subject," I say.

"You use angles all the time in hockey, though. Like when you're shooting the puck thingy at the goal, that's angles."

"I just point and shoot. Why are we talking about hockey? I thought you weren't a fan."

"I'm not *not* a fan. It's just not something I'm willing to commit three hours of my life to several times a week. Anyway, that's irrelevant.

I'm talking about our parents. I feel like they're way more serious than I realized, which means we might end up as stepsiblings and I think we need to come to terms with that possibility."

"Oh, right. Yeah. Well, next year is my draft year with the NHL, so depending on how fast they move, there's a chance I'll already be playing for the farm team by the time our parents take it to the next level. At most, we'll only have a few months of the whole stepsibling situation, which should be manageable. You'd have your own bathroom. Or maybe they'd convert the pool house for one of us."

"Oh, that'd be cool. I'm planning to go to a local college so I don't have to pay out the butt for housing and stuff. I don't want to rack up all kinds of education debt."

"What about the whole living away from home, party like it's your job part of college, though?"

"I'm a Mathlete. My idea of a good party includes pizza with lactose-free cheese and winning at competitive Sudoku."

"You're like the exact opposite of all the girls I hang out with." I take the bowl from her and do a half-assed job drying it.

She uses the back of her hand to push her glasses up her nose. "I feel like your hanging out and my hanging out are a lot different. I also feel like most of the girls you spend time with probably want to do a lot of not talking."

"That's super true," I agree.

"Ah, so you're a typical jock fuckboy."

I shrug. "I wasn't always. This year things changed."

"Your promising rise to hockey stardom made all the girls fall in lust with you?"

"Something like that." Mostly it was the whole teeth getting fixed thing and Randy forcing me to talk to girls, but the hockey situation is like teen girl catnip.

"It's weird that people feel the need to rub up on future stars like it's somehow going to make them a star by proxy." She hands me another dish. "Hockey players make good money, don't they?"

"Not as good as football, or baseball, or basketball, but still pretty good. I'm hoping I get a contract for a few million to start."

"A few million to start? Man, it's too bad I suck at all things sporty. Except hula hooping. I can hula hoop like nobody's business."

"It's a real skill."

"Too bad hip gyrating isn't a six-figure job. Although hip thrusting naked can apparently make lots of money. Not really a career path I want to entertain, but still viable for some."

"Wait. Are you talking about porn stars?" My eyes dart to her chest, which is covered by a t-shirt.

"That's a land mine topic we should step around."

"You brought it up."

"And I'm putting it away. If we end up as stepsiblings we should probably avoid talking about things like porn, unless I'm making fun of the fact that the girls you bring home sound like they're auditioning for a role in an adult film."

"That's fair. And probably accurate."

We finish up the dishes and Violet and Skye thank my dad for having them over. Skye hugs me and Violet gives me a fist bump. We stand on the front porch and wave as they drive away.

"You and Violet seemed to get along pretty well," Dad says.

"Yeah. She's cool. Like super nerdy, and has zero verbal filter, but she's got good stepsister potential."

His eyebrows dance on his forehead. "Stepsister potential?"

"You and Skye have been dating for months. You got us together for a family barbeque and bought filet mignon and you've been looking at vacations. I can count on one finger how many times that's happened in my life." I pat him on the shoulder. "I think they'll be good for us."

Dad smiles. "Good. I think so, too."

Chapter Fourteen

Just the Two of Us

Skye

"I can stay here on my own. I'll be fine." Violet taps her lip with the end of her pencil, but it almost goes up her nose.

"Honey, you're only sixteen."

"Legally you can leave me home on my own at fourteen," she argues.

"Grandma and Grandpa Hall would love for you to stay with them for the weekend." I haven't broached the subject with them, but they love having Violet over.

"Oh, hell no. I have tutoring all day Saturday and there's no way I'm spending Sunday playing Uno. I love Grandma and Grandpa, but they only watch bad sitcoms with laugh tracks. There has to be another option. What about Miller?"

"His grandparents are going to check in on him."

"But he gets to stay on his own?" She crosses her arms.

"He's seventeen, and he has hockey practice on Friday, Saturday, and Sunday."

"So why can't I stay over there? He's mostly an adult. That house is enormous. It's not like they don't have the room."

I purse my lips. "I don't know if that's the best idea."

"Why the heck not? I'm super responsible. He and I get along just fine."

"He's a teenage boy."

"So?"

"What if he invites his friends over?" It's a legitimate worry, considering my first introduction to Miller and his friend. Although that friend is in Toronto, getting ready for his first pro hockey season, so he won't be around to help Miller make bad choices.

"I have pepper spray. And I've taken self-defense lessons. I know to aim for the balls and then the throat and eyes. Please don't make me stay with Grandma and Grandpa. Their house smells like cooked cabbage and farts."

She's not wrong. It's not like my parents are all that old. I was barely in my twenties when I had Violet and they had me in their early twenties, but my dad loves sauerkraut, so the house always smells like bad gas. "Let me talk to Sidney."

Violet throws her arms around me. "Yay! Thank you. I'm responsible. And if anything goes sideways, I can always defect to Grandma and Grandpa's."

"I haven't said yes yet."

"Right. Of course. I'll hold my gratitude until after you've talked to your boyfriend."

* * * *

"No parties," Sidney says sternly.

"No parties." Miller gives his dad the thumbs up.

"No parties." Violet pushes her glasses up her nose.

"There's a three-friend limit. And under no circumstances are you to invite Cliff over."

"I know, Dad. He's still grounded anyway and probably will be until he graduates." Miller tucks his thumbs in his pockets and rocks back on his heels.

"There's money in the junk drawer if you need to order food. I picked up half a dozen pizzas and two of them are lactose free for you, Violet." Sidney smiles at my daughter.

"Thanks, Sid."

"And we packed ramen in your overnight bag," I remind her.

"I remember, thanks, Mom." She glances between us. "If you forget to tell us something, you can always text. Or call us relentlessly and leave messages. We won't set the house on fire."

"Don't forget to set the timer on the oven if you cook anything," I say. Violet and I often miss that step.

"Your grandma and grandpa will stop by sometime this weekend,"

Sidney warns.

"It's on the list on the fridge." Miller inclines his head toward it.

After another fifteen minutes of reinforcing rules, Sidney and I are in his SUV, driving toward the lake district. It's only a couple hours away. The perfect distance for a weekend getaway. Far enough that we're out of reach of the city, but not so far that we can't come home in case of an emergency.

"They'll be fine, right?" Sidney asks.

"Of course they will. Violet is exceptionally responsible." And Miller isn't even remotely her type. Violet isn't into hockey playing jocks. And she's mentioned more than once that she thinks he might be part yeti with how much fuzz he has. I hadn't noticed, but then I'm pretty preoccupied with his dad. I did notice, however, how tough it is for him not to stare at her rack whenever we go over for a swim. Although, boobs have hypnotizing powers where teen boys are concerned.

"It's not Violet I'm worried about," Sidney mutters.

I run my fingers through the hair at his nape. Goosebumps rise and he makes a deep, appreciative sound. "Violet is good at keeping things under control. It'll be fine. And your parents are checking in on them."

My phone buzzes with a message. From Violet.

> *House is still standing. Miller drove me to tutoring which was nice. He went the speed limit and stopped completely at all stop signs. He also drives with his hands at ten and two and stopped for two rogue squirrels. All is well. Enjoy your weekend. Leave all the doors open if you want.*

I squint at my phone.

> *I can feel you giving me the stink eye. YOU left the door open and I will never let you live it down. Ever. Or until I do something similar in half a decade or possibly longer, depending on when guys are no longer idiots. Gotta go. Tutors be tutoring.*

"Everything okay?"

"Yup. Miller drove her to her tutoring and stopped at all the stop signs. We're good to enjoy a weekend without teens."

"Great." He taps on the steering wheel. "As soon as we get there, I vote we have sex on the first available surface."

"I am fully on board with that plan."

Sidney clears his throat. "I saw my doctor this week."

"Oh, is everything okay?" Sidney is in great shape. Even when I'm on top, I don't have to do much work.

"Yeah." He nods and does some more finger tapping. "I got a few blue pills, though."

"Blue pills?" All I can think of is The Matrix, or Alice in Wonderland.

"For longevity." His eyes dart down.

Mine follow. He's tenting the front of his khaki shorts impressively. "But you don't have problems with longevity."

"No. We rarely have time for more than two rounds, and I wanted to make sure I could perform should we decide we need to spend most of the weekend with my cock inside you."

Everything below the waist clenches and my nipples tighten. "Oh God, so few holes, so many hours to fill them all."

His grip on the steering wheel tightens and the vinyl squeaks under his palms. "How much longer until we get there?"

"Forty-five minutes."

He rolls his neck on his shoulders. "I might have to risk a speeding ticket so we can get started sooner."

I cross and uncross my legs. "I don't think I allowed myself to consider too closely what forty-eight uninterrupted hours would look like with you."

"We can spend as much or as little time naked as you want. I just felt it was important to be able to take care of all your needs whenever you wanted, however you wanted."

Chapter Fifteen

Rise to the Occasion

Sidney

Skye makes a good point about it taking longer to get to our destination if we get pulled over by the cop, so instead of driving like we're in the Indy 500, I go a respectable eight miles an hour over the speed limit and get us to the secluded cabin in the woods in thirty-seven minutes instead of forty-five.

I've been dealing with a half hard-on the entire drive, so the second the vehicle is in park, I wrench the door open. "Leave everything. We'll deal with it after I've fucked at least two orgasms out of you."

Skye scrambles to get her seatbelt undone and nearly falls out of the truck in her haste. I'm glad we're on the same page.

It takes me three tries to punch in the lock code, in part because Skye's already working on my belt and her fingers keep grazing my hypersensitive erection. It's tough to focus, but I finally get the combination right and we stumble across the threshold, lips already fused.

"A whole forty-eight hours with no interruptions," Skye pants against my lips.

Her hands are everywhere. One dips down to tackle the button on my shorts, the other slides into the hair at my nape.

"I've been concocting endless fantasies about all the ways I want to have you." I find the zipper on her sundress and pull it down.

She pushes the straps over her shoulders, exposing a devastatingly sexy pink lace bra. I kiss and nibble a path from her throat, down to the valley of her lush, ample breasts. "God, I wanna fuck these glorious tits later."

"First you have to pound my pussy until she weeps."

I bite the swell on a groan. "I love your filthy, naughty mouth."

"Good, because it's only going to get naughtier the more hours we spend naked. Unless I'm choking on your cock or gargling your balls." She shoves her hand down the front of my shorts and wraps her warm, soft fingers around my length.

I'm rock solid and ready to fuck.

"Knock, knock! It's your friendly neighbor popping by!" A female voice singsongs from the other side of the door. It's followed by a beat being rapped on the door.

"Are you fucking kidding me?" I groan.

"Hellooooo! You left your keys in your car and your door open!" She trills again and follows with the same knocking beat.

My cock is raging.

"I'll deal with this. Why don't you give yourself a minute in the bathroom to handle things?" Skye releases my desperately hard cock, tucks it back in my boxers and gives it a there-there pat. "But don't actually handle things. I want to do that."

"My balls literally ache," I gripe.

"I'll give them a mouth massage later. After you slap them against my pussy. I'll take care of the neighbor."

I blow out a frustrated breath. "To be continued." I wander down the hall, holding my aching junk while Skye pulls her dress back into place and fluffs her hair before throwing open the door.

"Howdy neighbor!" she exclaims.

I find a bathroom on the right and duck inside, but don't close the door. The window is open, so I can listen to their conversation. I check out my cock. The head is an angry purple color, and the tip is weeping.

"Oh hi! I thought maybe you'd disappeared down to the lake. I live just next door. I wanted to stop by and introduce myself. Last week, the owners rented this place to a bunch of twenty-somethings, and they blasted awful music all week and all I could smell was the devil's lettuce. You left your keys in your car." A faint jingle follows.

"Thanks so much. My boyfriend has some gastrointestinal distress, and he made a mad dash to the bathroom. He's lactose intolerant and I guess there was dairy in whatever he ate when we stopped for lunch. He'll be tied to the porcelain throne for the next few hours. And you don't have to worry about music or the devil's lettuce. We're celebrating our anniversary. After he recovers from the gastro issues, anyway. Nothing a little Pepto and a couple hours of scrolling nonsense on the internet while bowing to the porcelain throne won't fix."

"Oh. Right. Okay. Well, that's...more than I really needed to know. I'll just leave you to settle in. I hope your boyfriend feels better soon."

"Once he exorcises the demons from his bowels, I'm sure he'll be fine. Thanks for stopping by!"

The door closes and I catch some muttering, but not the content as our nosy neighbor treks back through the trees to her own place.

I step into the hallway in time to watch Skye's dress drop to the floor. "Now where were we?"

"By the sound of it, I'll be in the bathroom for the next several hours."

"We can absolutely have sex in the bathroom if that's where you want to start." She flicks the clasp on her bra. Her boobs bounce free as the straps slide down her arms.

"This hallway looks good to me." I pop the button on my shorts and shove them down my thighs, boxer briefs and all.

Skye shimmies out of her panties.

I yank my shirt over my head and toss it on the floor.

Skye sighs. "My God, you are every fantasy I've ever had and more. Bring that dick over here so I can hop on and go for a joy ride."

I do a half squat, grab her by the ass, and hoist her up. Her nails dig into my shoulders as she scrambles for purchase and she tries to hook her legs around my waist, but she kicks the wall.

"Ow! Fuck!"

"Are you okay?" I readjust my grip.

"Just clumsy. I'll be fine. Let's get this fuck party started. I better have a hard time walking by the end of the weekend."

"I can absolutely make that happen."

She hooks one arm around my neck and gropes between us with her free hand. Her fingers wrap around my aching cock and we both groan. "My pussy is ready for one hell of a pounding."

"God, I love your filthy mouth," I grunt.

"You can fuck it later," she promises.

She runs the head over her clit and lines us up. We stopped using condoms a couple months in because Skye has an IUD. I loosen my hold and she sinks down, encasing me in velvety, wet warmth.

"I really love your cock, Sid. So fucking much."

"I know. You tell me every time you're about to come on it. But it never hurts to hear it again." Skye is a very vocal, very fun partner. She never leaves me guessing.

"I'd need a ball gag in order to keep my feelings to myself." She rolls her hips.

I press her against the wall for leverage, between two paintings of what is presumably the lake we're currently on. There's a chair rail that's the perfect height for her to grab onto. She wraps one hand around the narrow lip and keeps the other hooked around the back of my neck.

"Ready for a pussy pounding?"

"So goddamn ready."

I pull my hips back until I reach the ridge and wait until Skye's eyes flutter open before I fill her again. She moans and clenches around my cock.

"Tight like a fucking fist," I grunt.

"My ego loves you."

I pull my hips back and push in again, harder this time.

Skye's nails dig into my shoulder and her thighs shake. "Thank God we're not relying on me for longevity."

"You gonna come already, baby?"

"The drive was like ninety minutes of foreplay."

I pull out to the ridge again and look down between us. My cock glistens and the insides of Skye's thighs are already wet. "You gonna make a big mess for me to clean up?"

"Probably. I'm sorry in advance."

"I'm not." I fill her again, hard and fast.

She throws her head back on a moan, whole body going rigid as she comes in violent waves, shouting my name and a bunch of nonsense.

I wait until the shaking subsides, and she's able to do more than moan before I pull her away from the wall and carry her to the bedroom where I continue to pound into her, this time on the huge king bed.

"Did you take one of those blue pills?" she pants after orgasm number three.

"No, I've been practicing orgasming without ejaculating." I pull out and flip her onto her stomach, then fill her from behind, stretching out and bracketing her legs with mine.

"So you can have multiples now, too?"

"Sort of. I'm getting close to the limit, though. You think you can come for me one more time?"

"We'll have to change the bedding."

"I brought three extra sets of sheets."

"You are the best boyfriend in the world."

I kiss her sweaty shoulder and slide an arm under her, pulling her to her knees while I fold back on mine. I saved this position for last on purpose. Skye has a thing for my balls slapping the back of her thighs. It makes her come so hard she sees stars. I ram into her from behind, the wet sound of flesh hitting flesh accompanied by her moans and my grunts.

She shoves her face into a pillow and screams her way through her fourth and final orgasm. It's while her pussy clenches tight around my cock that I finally allow the orgasm I've been fighting to roll through me.

We collapse in a sweaty heap on the damp comforter.

Skye rolls over so she's facing me. She settles a damp palm against my cheek. "I love you."

"I love you, too."

"That was a really great way to start this weekend."

"It was."

"We need a shower."

"We do. Wanna cuddle for a few minutes first?"

"Absolutely. But can we roll over so I'm not lying in a wet spot?"

Chapter Sixteen

It Was a Good Idea at the Time

Skye

"Oh my God, I feel like I've been run over by a truck," I groan as I flop onto my back.

Sidney rolls to his side, a frown furrowing his sexy brow. His hair is a rumpled mess, he has sleep lines across his cheek and he looks damn well amazing. "Are you having a lactose reaction? I thought dinner was non-dairy."

"I'm not having a reaction to dairy. I'm having a reaction to all that physical exertion yesterday. Muscles I didn't even know existed hurt." Even adjusting my pillow hurts. "I don't know that I should attempt three-hour marathon sex at my age."

Sidney snorts. "You're not even forty, Skye. You're basically riding the tail end of your sexual peak, and you weren't complaining about the marathon sex last night."

"It seemed like a good idea," I mutter. "I need a Tylenol, or three. And maybe some electrolytes. And I highly recommend that you don't take another blue pill today unless you're down with voyeurism. Why do my forearms hurt this much? Even my eyebrows are sore."

Last night after dinner, which ended with me as dessert on the dining room table, I suggested Sidney take a little blue pill so we could keep the party going. I blame the orgasm brain and the entire bottle of prosecco I consumed for that ridiculous idea. Sidney performed just fine without the blue pill. Sidney on the blue pill was a three-hour joystick ride that was a lot of fun in the moment, but the aftermath is something else.

I probably need to do yoga more than once a month.

Sidney rolls off the bed and hops to his feet. He's gloriously naked. And hard. Which seems like it should be impossible considering the excessive amount of boning we did last night.

I throw an arm over my face. The movement makes me groan in pain. "Stop taunting me with your rippling abs and your boyfriend dick!"

"I'll be right back with painkillers and water." He saunters out of the bedroom, bare ass jiggling.

"I love you and your butt," I call after his retreating form.

"Same!" he calls back.

A minute later he returns with a glass of water, a Gatorade, and two extra-strength painkillers. "Why don't I put on a pot of coffee and we can start our morning with a soak in the hot tub? That might help ease some of the aches?"

"That sounds like a great idea."

"Good. But before I do that, I have one other suggestion."

"Okay, shoot." I down the painkillers and drain the water.

"Orgasms have analgesic properties."

"I'd need to be hella drunk to entertain anal."

Sidney laughs. "I'm not suggesting anal, baby. I'm suggesting I give you an orgasm. If nothing else, it'll take your mind off the aches for a few minutes." He arches a sexy brow.

"I'd be willing to test the effectiveness of that theory."

Twenty minutes and two oral orgasms later, Sidney and I are relaxing in the hot tub with travel mugs full of coffee spiked with Bailey's. I also have my Gatorade. The hot tub boasts an incredible view of the lake, and there's a lattice privacy barrier covered in blooming flowers, so we're hidden from the neighbors' view. I have a feeling, based on our introduction yesterday, that this is highly intentional.

"Looks like last night went smoothly for the kids," I say as I check my most recent message from Violet. She's already at tutoring and Miller is at hockey practice.

"I'm so glad they're getting along," Sidney replies.

"Me too. It just makes this so much easier, doesn't it?" I motion between us.

He smiles and stretches his arm across the back of the hot tub, fingers caressing my shoulder. "It definitely does. Miller will probably be out of the house this time next year, but it's good to know he and Violet can co-exist in the same space peacefully. You know, for future weekend getaways."

I grin. "Sounds like you're already planning more of these."

"Absolutely."

* * * *

We spent most of the day down at the dock, basking in the sun and taking dips in the lake. It's a beautiful, relaxing day, and it's amazing to have alone time with Sidney.

In the evening we make dinner together—I manage the parts that don't require careful monitoring—and we sit outside under the covered gazebo. It's incredibly romantic with the string lights lining the roof, the small lanterns flickering their fake flames, and the sun setting on the lake.

"This weekend has been absolutely perfect." I rest my cheek on his biceps.

Sidney kisses the top of my head. "I can think of one thing that would make it better."

"Oh? What's that? And don't say anal."

He chuckles. "I swear I just slipped that one time. I wasn't actually trying to get into door two."

"Uh huh."

He kisses me chastely and stands. "I'll be right back. Don't go anywhere."

"What about that thing that would make this weekend more than perfect?" I call as he disappears inside.

"I'm getting it. I'll be right back."

He passes through the kitchen and heads down the hall.

I check my phone for new messages from Violet while I wait for Sidney. She's at Toby's for an impromptu Mathlete's meeting because Toby and Michael are having a freak out about their upcoming competition, but otherwise everything is fine. I'm just so grateful she's such a responsible young woman.

Sidney reappears a few minutes later with a silver bucket and a bottle of what looks like champagne and two fluted glasses.

"Champagne? You sure you're not angling for butt stuff tonight?"

"For someone who says she's so against it, you sure bring it up an awful lot, babe."

"I do, don't I?"

"Mm. We can come back to that. Later. After you've had a couple glasses of champagne." He winks and sets the ice bucket on the table, then rounds it so he's standing in the sunset's halo.

He adjusts my chair and then drops to one knee in front of me.

"I don't know if outdoor sexy times is a good idea. I'm not particularly quiet and I worry that my screaming might scare people into believing there are wolves lurking close by."

He grins. "Head out of the gutter for a minute, babe."

He pulls a small velvet box from his pocket.

"Oh!" I slap a hand over my mouth. "Oh my God. Is that what I think it is?"

"It's not a cock ring."

I slap his chest. "And you're on me about getting my head out of the gutter!"

"I love you."

"I love you, too, Sid, so much. I can't believe this is happening. I mean, it's the perfect setting, but I really didn't expect this. Okay. I'm shutting up because I'm ruining this." I bite my lips together.

"I know we haven't been together all that long, but I can't imagine my life without you, Skye. I've been looking for you for a long time, and now that I have you, I want to spend the rest of our lives falling in love over and over again. I want to fall asleep beside you and wake up next to you. I want lazy Sundays where I watch hockey and you try to distract me by wearing low cut tops. I want to remind you to take lactose pills when we go out for dinner, so you don't have to deal with gastro demons. I want the ups and down and everything in between. I just want you, Skye, and everything that comes with you. I want you to be my wife, but more than that, I want us to be a family. Will you marry me?"

"Oh my God, yes, Sid. Yes, I'll marry you. I'm a terrible cook, but I give great blow jobs, so I hope that balances things out."

We both laugh and I choke back a sob as he flips the lid open. Nestled in the velvet is a gorgeous ring with a huge rock of a diamond. It twinkles magnificently in the waning sun.

"Wow. This is just. Wow! It's gorgeous, Sidney. Just stunning." I hold out a trembling hand.

"I hope it's not too much." He lifts it from the cushion, his own hands shaking as he takes mine.

"It's ridiculous and perfect."

He slides the ring on my finger when a spider the size of a freaking softball descends from the roof above, heading straight for our outstretched hands.

"Oh my God! Holy shit!"

"Oh fuck, that thing is huge!" Sidney shouts when it reaches eye level.

I don't think about what I'm doing. I instinctively react, yanking my hand free of his. My chair topples over and I do a very uncoordinated backwards somersault while screaming my damn head off. I hop to my feet and almost roll my ankle while I continue to shriek like a banshee.

Sidney, being the much more reasonable of the two of us, yanks off his flip-flop and slams it on the table repeatedly until the giant spider is nothing but an obscenely large splatter mark.

"Is it dead?" I peer at the green and black smear on the brown tile and glance up. "Are there more?" I succumb to a whole-body shudder and hop back again.

"It's very dead and I don't think there are more." Sidney glances up and does the same shuddery thing. "At least I hope not. Way to fuck up my proposal, asshole," he mutters at the smear.

He pats his pockets and then looks at me expectantly. "Do you have the ring? Can we try that again? But maybe inside this time?"

I look down at my naked hand and back up at him. "Um." I glance around the deck. The sun is heading for the horizon in a hurry. We only have a handful of minutes of daylight left. I hold up my ringless finger. "I don't have it."

"Fuck." He runs his hand through his luxurious hair.

We scour the deck, but the spaces between the boards are the perfect width for a ring to fit through.

"Please tell me it didn't fall through one of those cracks."

"I'll go down and check." Sidney puts his flip-flop back on.

"I'll grab flashlights." I rush inside and search the cottage for flashlights. I find two, but they die two seconds after I turn them on, so I have to search for batteries. Five minutes later, I join Sidney under the deck. It's not tall enough for either of us to stand up fully, so we hunch uncomfortably.

"Any luck?" Asking is pointless. If he'd found it, I'd already know.

"Not yet. The flashlights should help." He shines his on the ground and something small scuttles away.

I scream and slam my head on a joist. "Ah! Shit. That's going to leave a bruise."

"Why don't you just wait inside, babe? I can handle this," Sidney offers.

"I should help. I'm the one who freaked out."

We spend the next ten minutes scouring the space under the deck for my brand-new engagement ring that I haven't even had a chance to wear yet. I hope this isn't a sign.

The sun has almost completely set by this point and I'm thirty seconds away from hysterical tears, when Sidney shouts, "I found it! It's here!"

"Yay! Thank God!" The tears of joy stream down my face. I just want to get out from under this deck where I'm sure a million eight-legged creatures and four-legged ones reside.

"Oh shit," he mutters.

"Oh shit, what?" My heart sinks.

"It literally fell into a pile of shit. Fuck a duck."

"I'll grab a napkin." I turn and rush toward the opening and slam my head a second time on a joist. "Ow! Fuck!"

"Babe, are you okay?" His flashlight swings my way.

"I'm fine. Just clumsy. Keep your eye on the ring. I'll be right back." I rush up the stairs, grab a napkin and rush back down, nearly falling again, but I manage not to slam my head against anything else. I hand Sidney the napkin and he retrieves my poop covered ring.

We head back up to the cottage.

After a thorough cleaning, we decide its best if we leave the ring to soak in some disinfectant. I have a bruise on my forehead and another significant bump on top of my head.

"That did not go the way I'd planned," Sidney inspects the bump on my forehead.

"I don't think either of us expected a spider the size of a bloated testicle to drop from the sky right in the middle of your proposal, or for the ring to land in the only pile of shit under the deck."

"I feel like that was punishment for killing the spider."

We both shudder.

"Maybe we should not talk about that. And also have a shower. And maybe some engagement-post-traumatic-event-distraction sex."

"I think all of those things sound great."

"And then we should drink that bottle of champagne, but I vote you go outside to get it."

"I can do that. Shower first, though?"

"Absolutely."

He links our fingers and tugs me down the hall. "At least we have an exciting story to tell at the wedding, right?"

Chapter Seventeen

I Should Have Known Better Part Two

Violet

On Friday evening I tutor until nine-thirty. Is it riveting for my social life? Nope. But it's great for my bank account. One of my fellow tutorees drives me back to Miller's house when our sessions are over. Miller isn't home when I get there, but that's not a surprise. He has hockey practice and then a game tomorrow morning, so I don't expect to see much of him this weekend.

The house has an alarm and cameras outside and stuff, and it's in a classy neighborhood, so I feel okay about being in it by myself. I tutor at eight-thirty Saturday morning with a kid who hates math more than I hate the moops, so I get ready for bed and call it a night early.

When I wake up the next morning Miller's already gone for hockey and I take the bus to the tutoring center.

I'm lulled into a false sense of security by the peacefulness of Friday night, but when I return to the Butterson residence late Saturday evening—I went to Toby's after tutoring for an impromptu Mathlete's meeting. We have a competition next week and it's against the first-place team. Toby and Michael are both freaking out—it's a completely different story. Music blasts through the outdoor stereo system, along with a girl-shrieking accompaniment.

I let myself into the house and find the living room full of high school couples in various stages of making out. The backyard seems equally full of rowdy teens. I scan the room for my future-stepbrother, but I don't see his fuzzy aura anywhere. Which is a problem.

I decide to check my temporary bedroom and am disgusted to find a couple boning on the bed I no longer plan to sleep in later.

Nothing of value is in the room, so I leave them to their grunting and groaning and continue my search for Miller. His bedroom door is locked. I knock but get no answer. I scope out the house, but it's strangers, strangers, and more strangers.

When I finally find Miller, it's clear he's been drinking. A lot. He stumbles over to me, doing some weird wave thing with his whole body. It reminds me of the inflatable balloon guy, except he pairs it with gun fingers and the contents of his red plastic cup slosh all over his hands. "Vi! Hey! You're here! I invited a few friends over. I hope you don't mind. Don't tell my dad."

"You're friends with the entire population of your high school?" I ask.

He slings one meaty arm around my shoulder. His damp armpit rests on my unfortunately exposed skin. "I'm a social blubberfly," he slurs.

"Kick ass party, Buck. Who's your friend?" A dude-bro swagger weaves over and leers at my tank top covered chest.

"This is Vi, she's gonna be my stepsister. Vi, this is Jeff, I mean Jordy," Miller squints at his friend. "He's my good buddy."

I wave. Then turn back to my drunk future stepbrother. "Can I talk to you for a minute?"

"Yeah. Of course. Anyfing for you." He does a thumbs up dance for his friend. "We'll be back."

I duck out from under his arm. Miller's ability to walk in a straight line is highly compromised, so I take his elbow and lead him to the pool house.

No less than six people call him Buck on the way.

It's moderately quieter in the pool house and there are no bodies fornicating, which is a relief. "Why is everyone calling you Buck?"

"It's what all my friends call me. You should call me that, too, actually. Only my dad calls me Miller."

"But why?" The only connection I can make is to a bucking bronco. Which might fit.

He pulls on his front teeth and suddenly they're in his hand and his mouth is sporting a black gap where they used to be.

"What in the actual fuck?"

"I got a puck to the face last year. Best thing that ever happened to me. Knocked out my front teeth, so now I have these fakies until I can get implants."

"I still don't get the nickname."

"It's a joke. Everyone knows me as Buck around here. Just roll with it."

I rub the back of my neck. "Uh, okay then, Buck. You realize there are people making out all over your house, right?"

He looks confused. "I thought I locked the screen door."

"There are people fucking in my bed."

"Oh shit. Really? I'll get them out."

I grab his wrist before he bolts for the door. He's way stronger than I am, though, so he drags me along for a few steps. "Wait!"

He comes to an abrupt halt, and I slam into him. His eyes are wide and mostly vacant. He's so wasted. This is not good.

"How many of these people do you know?"

He shrugs. "Most of them are from my school or my hockey team."

"And the rest of them?"

He shrugs.

"Not to be a total downer, but you realize we have to clean up this mess tomorrow, right?" And based on his inability to focus on my face for more than two seconds, I'll be doing the lion's share of the work involved. Unless I throw him under the bus. That's looking more appealing the longer I watch him do a weeble wobble impression.

"It's cool. I'll take care of it." He blinks repeatedly. "Let's get those fuckers out of your room."

I have little confidence in his ability to put one foot in front of the other, let alone get people to stop banging in my temporary room, but I follow him across the patio, anyway.

He falls into the pool on the way. Which is not a surprise. It helps sober him up a little. He's accosted by no fewer than four girls in the pool. He strips down to his boxer briefs. Unfortunately, they're white, so I'm treated to the very clear outline of his peen when he drags himself out of the water.

He continues across the backyard, undeterred, apparently. Again, he's stopped several times by girls who are very excited by his wet boxers. Eventually, by some miracle, we make it to the house. He drips all over the floor as we pass through the kitchen. He nabs an open bag of chips on the way and shoves his giant mitt in the bag, cramming a handful of chips into his face, half of which end up on the floor. When we reach the living room, there are three couples going at it on various pieces of furniture.

I don't know what kind of high school he goes to, or whether I'm just extraordinarily sheltered, because I've never seen so many exhibitionist teenagers in my entire life. Although I am a Mathlete, and I did accidentally teach one of my teammates how to French kiss without using too much tongue. Because he and Abby are still dating, and I've heard rumors about his exceptional kissing skills, I feel justified in taking some credit for that, even if the whole situation was cringey and awkward.

"Hold this for me." Miller, or Buck, or whatever I'm supposed to call him, hands me the bag of chips.

He cups his hands around his mouth. "Hey! No fucking on my living room furniture! Take it to the backyard." Chips fly out of his mouth and land on the floor. He wipes his hands on his chest, smearing wet chip crumbs all over his abs and his blond fuzz.

He's living up to the jock stereotype in spectacular fashion.

He's a decent guy. But when all these dude-bros get together, their combined testosterone levels reduce their brain function to ten percent.

The couples break apart and hands duck out of tops and bottoms. I don't want to contemplate too closely the bodily fluids that are currently being wiped on Sidney's sofa. All the horny teens vacate the living room.

Buck-Miller takes the bag of chips from me, and I follow him upstairs. When we get to my temporary bedroom, he throws open the door. I'll never be able to unsee the tangle of limbs, or the frankly disturbing act taking place on my bed.

"Is she eating his a—"

Miller-Buck's hand comes up to cover my eyes. I'm semi-grateful, because I couldn't look away and I honestly didn't want to see any more of that, but my eyeballs refused to close.

"Get the fuck out!" he bellows.

There's a flurry of motion, which I don't see because Buck-Miller's giant mitt blocks my view.

"Sorry, Buck," the guy mutters as they pass, still both naked and carrying their clothes.

Buck drops his hand once they're gone. The room smells like butt.

"I feel like just standing here will give me pinkeye."

"You can stay in my room tonight and I'll sleep in here," Buck offers.

"The sheets need to be changed." I don't want to touch them.

"I'll sleep in my dad's room," he amends. "Come on."

I follow him down the hall. He unlocks his door. His room is a typical teenage guy mess. Clothes hang over his computer chair and litter the floor around his bed and by his dresser and closet. A box of tissue and a giant bottle of lotion sit on his nightstand. The garbage can beside his bed is full of used tissue.

"I don't know if your bed is any better than the one in my room," I observe.

"I changed my sheets this morning."

I side-eye him.

"Swear on my mom's grave." He makes the sign of the cross.

My heart twinges at that. My mom told me he lost his mom to a rare brain tumor when he was just three.

"My friends think you're cute," he blurts. "They like the whole nerdy vibe you got going on." He makes a circle motion to my face.

"They probably think I'm all inexperienced and virginal. And I'm close to fun-sized with a rack." I motion unnecessarily to my boobs. "All plusses for the cisgender straight or bi identifying XYs."

"Are you inexperienced?" Buck's voice cracks.

"Teenage boys are idiots. My mom is pro-self-exploration."

"Whoa. Wait. What?" His eyes are comically wide. "You masturbate?" He sounds like he's regressed a few years and puberty has reclaimed him.

I roll my eyes and stalk across his room, pointing to his nightstand where exhibits A through C are located.

"Yeah, but I'm a dude. All dudes choke the chicken."

"So because I'm a girl, I'm not supposed to take care of my own needs?"

His unfocused gaze moves over me. "If you become my stepsister, you're forbidden. My teammates think that's cool."

I hold up both hands. "Stop right there. Whatever you're thinking about saying, keep it in your word hole. That path is closed. Never to be walked down. Ever. There are enough romance books out there about it, and that's where it should stay, in fiction."

"It'd be weird if we hooked up," he mutters.

"Our parents are dating and based on how things are going, there is a solid chance they'll get engaged, which means they'll get married, and then we'll be stepsiblings. The only things we have in common is that our parents are hot for each other and we're both in high school. From a statistical standpoint, the chances that we would work out in the long term are exceptionally low. Especially since you're heading for a career in professional hockey and a ridiculous number of girls have flirted with your exceptionally drunk ass since I got here tonight. And you seem to be a huge fan of the attention, which is understandable since you're a walking hormone. Based on these factors alone, it would be an extremely bad idea to hook up." I'm also not into the fuzzy blond jock type, but I leave that part unsaid.

"That's not. I didn't mean—" He turns around, grips the door jamb, and hurls all over the floor.

At least it's the hallway, and it's hardwood.

Chapter Eighteen

Not The Turn I Expected

Sidney

"It's just so pretty." Skye hasn't stopped smiling or staring at her ring.

"I'm glad you like it."

"I don't like it. I love it. It's beautiful." She shifts in her seat. "I can't believe I'm engaged. Should we tell the kids when we get home? Should we wait?"

"It's totally up to you." I set my hand palm up on the center console and she slips hers into mine. I bring it to my lips and kiss her knuckle. "Are we moving too fast? Should I have waited to pop the question until weekend away number two or three?"

"If you'd waited, we might not have such an exciting story to tell." Skye squeezes my hand.

"This is true. That was one hell of a night."

"I loved every moment, save the fifteen minutes between the spider and finding the ring."

"How's your head?" She has a minor bruise on her forehead that's covered by her hair and a significant lump on top.

"It's fine. Nothing a little concealer won't cover until it fades." She taps her lip. "I don't know if I'll be able to keep this news from Violet for very long. We're pretty open with each other."

"That's fair. Miller and I are the same. Why don't we see what the state of the house is, and if Miller and Violet have stayed friends? Then we can decide if we want to tell them right away," I suggest.

"Sure. That sounds good." Skye checks her phone and frowns.

"Violet still hasn't answered my text this morning."

"Maybe she's sleeping in? Miller sometimes plays video games all hours of the night. He could have wrangled Violet into playing them with him," I offer.

"It's possible. She did tutor all day yesterday and then she had a meeting with the Mathletes, so I'm sure she's exhausted."

An hour later, we drive down my street and Skye's hope that her daughter slept in because of all her math-ish endeavors fizzles. "Are those red plastic cups littering the lawn?"

"Miller better not have thrown a party while we were away or I'll ground him until he gets shipped off to training camp," I grumble as I turn into the driveway.

"Maybe someone else on the street threw a party," Skye's voice is high and nervous. The truck is still moving and her door is already open.

I shift into park and we both hop out, leaving our bags and the mostly empty cooler in the trunk.

Skye grabs my arm when we reach the hood of the SUV. "Oh God. Is that a used condom on the driveway? That looks like a used condom, Sidney."

I follow her gaze. An inch from her foot is a green condom. At least they had the decency to tie a knot in the end so the contents aren't splattered all over my interlock. But its location begs a lot of questions. As does the color. "It's a used condom," I regretfully agree.

"Oh God. Teenage parties are the worst. Violet better still be a virgin. All she's done so far is kiss a couple of boys. I need her to make good decisions until college, or hopefully later, when boys don't have their heads up their asses when it comes to finding the hot buttons." She releases my arm and stalks across the driveway, skirting around plastic cups and another condom.

My hands are unsteady as I unlock the door and usher Skye into the front hall. We're lulled into a false sense of security until we reach the kitchen and living room. The inside of the house looks far worse than I ever could have expected. Red plastic cups litter the counter and every other available surface. Chips bags and their contents are scattered across the floor. It smells like the inside of a brewery and a jockstrap. I spot at least two more condoms on the floor. Not in their wrappers. There are two boxes of condoms on the coffee table, both open.

Skye looks appropriately horrified as she calls out, "Violet?"

We glance at each other and rush for the stairs. She makes it to the spare room before I do. "Oh God. Oh, my God. She's not here!" She runs into the room and throws open the bathroom door. "She's not here! And there are condom wrappers on the floor! Oh God. Oh my God." She spins around and grabs my arms. "Where *is* she? What did she *do*? *What did I let happen?*"

"Maybe the used condom wrappers aren't hers," I say, unhelpfully.

"I don't know if that's better or not. Who was fucking in her bedroom then? And where is she? She hasn't texted since last night at ten-thirty. She said she was coming back here. And I've heard nothing from her since! What if she was kidnapped?" Panic has clearly taken over. It's understandable. Violet is a sweet, quirky, nerdy girl. At least at first. Once she's comfortable, her sassy side shows, and she comes out with some stunning one-liners.

"Let's check Miller's room. Maybe he knows where she is." He better know where she is, or he's grounded for the rest of his goddamn life.

"Yes. Okay. Yes. Let's do that." Skye nods compulsively and follows me down the hall to my son's room.

"Miller?" I knock twice. "I'm coming in."

I throw open the door.

The smell is the first thing to register. It's slightly sour, and definitely beer-y. It's only partially masked by the cologne. Miller is passed out in his bed, the sheets mostly thrown off. They cover him from waist to knee.

There's a body beside him. A small body. Although everyone looks small compared to my son. But this small body is also familiar. Horribly familiar.

"This isn't happening." Skye grabs my arm, nails digging into my skin. "Please tell me I'm hallucinating."

"We shouldn't jump to conclusions." My blood pressure feels like it's gone up a hundred points in the last five seconds.

If my son charmed my fiancée's daughter into his bed, I'm going to lose my ever-loving shit. Loudly.

Miller rolls over onto his back and the sheets shift with him. He's not wearing boxers. In fact, he's not wearing anything.

Chapter Nineteen

It's Not What It Looks Like

Miller

A siren blares. No. Wait. It's not a siren, someone is screaming my name. I blink a few times, but the brightness in the room, combined with the shouting, isn't great. I have the wickedest headache. My brain feels like it's being squeezed in a vise. It's awful.

"Stop the yelling," I mutter and try to put my pillow over my head, but it's yanked out of my hands.

"Oh shit! Oh my God! My eyes!" Violet shrieks. The bed jostles and there's a thud.

I blink a few times and glance toward the noise as Violet pops to her feet. She tosses a pillow at me, but it lands at my waist. She's not wearing her glasses and her hair is a wreck.

Which is when I realize we're in my bedroom and she just rolled out of my bed. And I'm completely naked.

"It's not what it looks like!" Violet says.

"You were in bed together and Miller is naked!" Skye yells.

My head throbs at her volume.

"He wasn't naked when we fell asleep. I swear! He was wearing a pair of shorts and a t-shirt," Violet shrieks.

Her face has turned red and there are blotchy patches on her neck and collarbones.

I have no idea what the hell is going on. My memories of last night are hella vague. I remember Cliff boning his sometimes-girlfriend in Violet's room. There may have been some weird shit going down. I also remember, vaguely, mentioning that Violet is forbidden fruit. Or something. Maybe that was in my head. I hope it was in my head. Unfortunately, it sounds like something I would say out loud, not on purpose.

As I slowly process the scene, I worry that I'm very wrong. Because I'm super naked and we're in the same bed and I'm not sure how we got here. I vaguely remember a couple of my teammates making comments about Violet. I also remember two girls yammering on about stepbrother romance and how it never really goes out of style. I didn't even know that was a thing, although in my defense, I typically avoid reading books because the words jump all over the fucking page on me.

I leave behind my confusing thoughts and tune back into what's going on around me, mostly because my dad is blowing a gasket.

"Why are you in bed together in the first place? And what the hell went on here last night? The house is a disaster. I told you, three friends over max. I want some answers! Now!" Dad booms.

I cover my ears with my palms and groan.

"I think maybe we should let Miller get dressed and then we can figure it out from there," Skye says. At least she's not shrieking anymore. That's good.

Her eyes are wide with shock and horror. Both are understandable. Especially if I accidentally drunk slept with my future stepsister. I really hope that isn't what happened. I hope there's a reasonable excuse for Violet being in my bed that doesn't include sex I can't remember.

Skye hustles Violet out of my bedroom, but Dad stays put. He closes the door and crosses his arms. I've done plenty of stupid shit in my life, including trying to get into a bar with Randy last year during one of our games up in Canada, but I've never seen him this angry in my life. It's fucking terrifying. It doesn't help that all I have is a pillow to shield my nakedness. I belatedly realize that both Violet and Skye have now seen my junk. And I was probably sporting a morning chub.

"Well?" Dad's right eye twitches.

I'm staring at my lap. I look at him for a second. "Huh?"

"Violet is sixteen fucking years old and my fi—girlfriend's daughter." His face is an uncomfortable shade of red.

"Maybe you should sit down. Or take an aspirin? Your face." I stop talking because the twitch in his eye is getting worse.

"Did you put your hands on her?"

"You mean, like, on her fun parts?" That was the very wrongest way to word that sentence, but it's already out of my mouth and I can't take it back.

"Did you engage in sexually inappropriate conduct with my girlfriend's daughter?" His voice is low and quiet, but not in a reassuring way. More in the he's a powder keg ready to blow way.

I open and close my mouth several times, but no words come out. Because I don't have the answer to that. I try to stealth like bring my fingers to my nose, because if I did do stuff with Violet, they should tell me. Or the smell should tell me.

Dad's eyes look like they're about to bug out of his head. For half a second, I imagine them shooting across the room and pinging around off the walls. I almost laugh. Almost.

Except before I can get my fingers within sniffing distance of my nose, my dad is right there, an iron grip around my wrist.

We stare at each other for a few long, horrible seconds. Because he knows what I was about to do. I feel like I'm about to hurl. And maybe cry.

"Did you touch Violet?" Dad grits from between clenched teeth.

I go with honesty. "I don't know." I need to talk to Violet. I don't think I would have done anything inappropriate, because I know how much my dad likes Skye. And I really like Skye, too. It's been nice having her around. She's the cool mom everyone loves because she says the things other moms won't. And I sincerely hope my stupidity hasn't fucked this all up for me and my dad.

"You don't *know*?" We both look at my hand.

He releases my wrist and takes a step back. His hands are shaking. His whole body is. And his eyes are still bugging. "How can you *not* know?"

I rub my nose.

Relief hits me like an anvil. My right hand smells like soap. "I'm pretty sure nothing happened."

"*Pretty sure?*"

The fingers don't lie. But it doesn't mean nothing, *nothing* happened. Just nothing below the waist. Jesus, I really hope nothing, *nothing* happened or I'm going to be grounded until I die.

I don't have a chance to answer because there's a soft knock on my bedroom door.

Chapter Twenty

I Cannot End My Only Son

Sidney

I think my head is going to explode. I have never been as angry at Miller as I am now. Not when he backed his friend's car into my truck and did three grand in damage to my tailgate two days after he got his driver's permit. Not when I found out he'd been using my truck to make out with his girlfriend after hockey practice, not even when he and Randy brought girl's home when I was on a date.

Or the time when he and Randy snuck out of the hotel during an away game and tried to go to a bar, but ended up getting picked up by the cops. Even if I put together every single one of those instances, and rolled all my anger into one giant ball, it wouldn't compare to the rage I'm rocking.

I point to my son. "Put some clothes on."

"Now?"

"Yes. Now."

He keeps the pillow in front of his junk and rushes over to his dresser. He grabs whatever is in the top drawer and hustles his bare ass into the bathroom. I wait until that door closes before I open the one behind me.

Skye is standing on the other side, looking beautiful and stressed. She glances to the right, toward the stairs. "I sent Violet to wait in the car. I'm going to take her home and get her side of this story. I feel like she's trying not to throw Miller under the bus. She's a horrible liar, though, so it shouldn't be too difficult to get to the bottom of things."

"Miller's changing. I'll talk to him and we can compare notes in a couple of hours?"

"That sounds reasonable." She wrings her hands.

"I'm so sorry, Skye." My stomach feels like it's trying to turn itself inside out.

"You didn't do anything wrong. I should have sent Violet to her grandparents for the weekend." She taps her lips with her fingers. I notice her engagement ring is no longer decorating the important one. "Let's put telling the kids about the other thing on hold until we get to the bottom of this."

I'm trying not to panic. Or read into that any more than necessary. It makes sense to deal with this situation before we tell them we're engaged. My big worry is that Miller has a thing for nerdy types. He's proven that by getting fresh with his tutors this year. I can overlook him making out with whoever is helping him with his English essays. But if my son and Skye's daughter hooked up this weekend, it will make moving forward with this relationship difficult. Maybe impossible.

She pats me on the chest, her smile reflecting the same unease churning in my gut. "We'll get this figured out. I'll call you later."

I notice she doesn't placate me with bullshit like everything is going to be okay. Because it might not be. I feel sick. I nod instead of answering with words.

I should make an appointment with my therapist after this, regardless of the outcome. Because as Skye and I have a silent conversation in which all our fears play out on our faces, I realize that I'm beyond in love with her. I've already planned out my future and she's in every single fictional fantasy. I want to get old with her, get wrinkly and soft, spoil grandkids, and enjoy retirement with her. But all that seems to hang in the balance of whatever did or didn't happen while we were away this weekend.

She breaks eye contact first and disappears down the stairs.

The bathroom door opens. Miller looks like he's just as at risk of vomiting as I am.

I cross my arms. "You're grounded forever."

He nods once. His jaw works, like he's trying not to cry. He wrings his hands, eyes wide and darting around. "Is Violet still here? Maybe I need to talk to her."

"She and Skye went home."

He rolls his lips between his teeth. "Is she okay?"

"You honestly don't remember anything? Do you understand how problematic that is?"

He nods again. "I only invited a few of the guys over. But then one of them wanted to invite his girlfriend. And I should've said no, but I didn't. And then it snowballed from there. And someone's brother brought a bunch of hard liquor over and well…things got out of hand." He rubs the back of his neck.

I cross my arms. "There are condom wrappers all over the floor in the spare bedroom, where Violet was supposed to be sleeping." Maybe Skye shouldn't have left. Maybe this would have been better managed with all of us together, instead of the divide and conquer, especially since my son is having issues remembering what in the sweet shit took place last night.

His already white face turns green. He spins around and dives into the bathroom, retching like he's exorcizing an entire team of demons from his stomach.

His phone buzzes from somewhere on the floor. I search through the random clothes strewn across the hardwood and see nothing that belongs to a girl, which is a relief.

I finally find his phone in a pair of shorts that somehow made their way under his bed. The most recent message was sent a minute ago from Violet.

I stalk to the bathroom, where Miller is hugging the toilet bowl. "I'm so sorry, Dad. I'm so sorry. I didn't mean to throw a party. It was just supposed to be a couple friends. And I didn't mean to get drunk like that. It won't ever happen again. Oh God." He heaves again. "I don't think anything happened. I really hope nothing happened. I really like Skye. I kinda hoped she'd end up being my stepmom and that Violet would be my stepsister. And I know that would make her totally off limits. Sober me knows that she's forbidden. Oh, shit." He hurls again. "I think I might have said that to her."

Between heaves I snap my fingers and use his momentary distraction to unlock his phone with facial recognition. I click on the message from Violet.

> *I'm trying not to throw you under the bus, but the house is in shambles, so that's a hole you'll have to dig yourself out of. Not sure what they think happened last night. I like yetis, but only as cute characters in movies or stuffies. Hope your hangover doesn't kill you before your dad does.*

Chapter Twenty-One

Oh, Thank God

Skye

The stomach issues from this whole nightmare are going to be legendary. My hands are shaking as I climb into the driver's seat and turn the engine over. It isn't until I've pulled out onto the street that Violet speaks.

"Can I say something now?"

Every time she's tried to speak I've told her it had to wait until we were in the car. "I need you to be honest with me."

"Last night I came back to Sid's after the emergency Mathlete's meeting in which both Toby and Michael had full on meltdowns that included hyperventilating, which was fun, and the house was full of Buck's friends. And apparently they call him that because his front teeth are missing. I think it's supposed to be some kind of joke. Anyway, he was wasted and so were all his idiot friends. I mean, I guess a few of them probably weren't idiots, but the booze definitely impacted the level of stupidity going on last night. It was a shitshow."

"The red plastic cups and the horrible number of condoms made that pretty clear," I grind out.

"I've never witnessed so much exhibitionism in my life."

"Oh my God. Your innocence is gone," I lament.

"Maybe we should stop and get me a milkshake. I don't know that driving while having this conversation is the best idea," Violet says.

I try to strangle the steering wheel. "Did anything happen between you and Miller? He was *naked*."

She points to the right and I pull into the drive thru line up. There are four cars ahead of us.

"When I put Buck to bed last night he was wearing shorts and a t-shirt. But I imagine he gets pretty hot with all that fuzz he's sporting."

"Why did you put him to bed? And what were you doing in his bed in the first place?" My voice is too loud. A teenage couple entering the restaurant stop to stare for a second. I roll up my window.

"Can you stop yelling? I'm two feet away. I get that you're freaking out, but I feel like maybe the volume doesn't need to be so high." Violet pushes her glasses up her nose.

I drop my volume to a reasonable level. "I just need some answers, Violet."

"I know. I'm trying to explain. Like I said, Buck was a mess. He started talking a bunch of nonsense and ended up throwing up all over the hallway. It was disgusting. I had to clean it up. And then he spent another twenty minutes in the bathroom regurgitating everything he'd put in his stomach, which was excessive and repulsive, but at least that stuff was flushable."

"Move the story forward, Violet."

"Right. Yeah. Anyway, I had to get all these people out of the house, which took freaking ages. Buck passed out in the bathroom for a while and then I finally got him into his bed, which was a feat because he's huge and I'm me." She points to herself.

We pull up to the drive thru and Violet orders half the menu. I pay for the obscene amount of food I'm sure she'll never finish and then wait as the line of cars moves forward at what feels like a snail's pace.

"So I get him into bed and I make sure he's lying on his side, because that's what you're supposed to do with intoxicated people."

"How do you know that's what you're supposed to do?"

"I learned it in health class, maybe? Or when I took that Red Cross course? Anyway, drunk people aren't supposed to sleep on their backs because they could asphyxiate on their own vomit. And while the whole party thing was horrible to come home to, I think a slightly trashed house is highly preferable to something like that happening. But Buck kept rolling over onto his back. So I kept having to roll him back onto his side. Which means I had to stay awake until, like, six in the morning, monitoring him and making sure he didn't die. He owes me so big." She crosses her arms and waits as we pull forward and the drive-thru kid passes over three enormous bags.

I pull over and park. "So, nothing happened between you and

Miller?"

Violet wrinkles her nose. "You mean other than me cleaning up his vomit and making sure he made it through the night?" She opens the first bag and pulls out a breakfast tray of pancakes. "Man, I'm hungry."

"He was naked."

"Can we not keep bringing that up? Buck's dangler is the last thing I want to think about when I'm about to eat a maple syrup dipped sausage." She spears a sausage link with a fork.

"So all you did was make sure he was okay? That's it?" I'm still gripping the wheel so tightly my knuckles are white.

"*That's it?*" Violet stops with the fork half an inch from her mouth. "I had to prod a hundred teenage hornballs out of the house and the yard, clean up the mess he made in the hallway, and stayed up until six in the morning to make sure he didn't die. I feel like 'that's it' is downplaying how kickass of a stepsister I'm gonna be." She takes a hearty bite of sausage link while glaring at me.

"So nothing sexual happened?" I ask.

"What?" Violet flails and her sausage link goes flying, as do her pancakes. The syrup flips over and lands on her leg, then slides down her shin and hits the floor. A pancake lands on the dashboard and another lands on the center console. "Oh my God! Ew! No!" she gags dramatically. "Seriously, mom? Did you miss the part where he hurled all over the hallway? Or the part where I'm vying for top spot as stepsister of the fucking millennium? You're dating his freaking dad, who might end up being my stepdad. There is a less than zero percent chance I would ever entertain that scenario. Also, he's not even remotely my type. Nothing against hockey players, but they all seem to be relentless horndogs and my energy is currently funneled into getting into a great college, not fumbling my way through lackluster sexual experiences with dude-bros." She looks down at her lap. "Jesus. Why am I covered in pancakes and syrup?"

"Oh, thank God." I release the steering wheel and burst into tears.

"Mom? Are you okay? What's wrong?"

I try to reassure her, but it comes out as a relieved sob.

"Mom? Ma? Mummy?"

I hold up a hand and shake my head.

"Did you honestly believe something happened between me and Buck? I feel like I have to call him Buck instead of Miller until the end of time now. Wait. Is this because you've been reading those smutty stepbrother romance novels again in your book club?"

I get myself under control enough to say, "He was naked."

"I was fully clothed. And his room smelled like vomit and dirty socks."

"I panicked."

"Clearly," I say.

I hand Violet a napkin.

It sticks to her fingers, so she uses the bottom of her shirt instead.

"I need a shower, and your car needs to be detailed. I have no idea where that sausage went, either."

"Why don't we go home and get cleaned up?" I need half an hour to get over this before I call Sidney.

"That seems reasonable."

I pull out of the spot while Violet cleans her hand with a wet wipe and then digs around in another bag, producing a container of french fries.

"I can't believe you actually thought something happened with me and Buck," she muses as she pops a fry into her mouth. "He's got a lot of chest hair for a seventeen-year-old and, logically speaking, he's only going to get fuzzier with time and hormones. Also, that he takes out his front teeth to entice random girls is a little weird."

Her phone buzzes and she spends the next minute trying to find it. "Buck texted me." She frowns and pops another fry into her mouth as she reads the message.

"What did he say?"

"Oh, this is interesting," Violet mumbles.

"Interesting how? What did Buck say?"

"He apologized, then asked what happened last night, and followed it up by saying he hopes he didn't do or say anything inappropriate."

"So he doesn't remember? Poor Sid. I need to call him. He must be losing his mind. Apparently Buck is a real Casanova."

Violet snorts. "I don't know if I'd go that far." She punches in a message in response.

"Are you messaging him back? What are you saying?"

"That he owes me for making sure he didn't die last night, and that he didn't do anything inappropriate." She pops another fry into her mouth. "I would have made him sweat a little longer if I didn't feel bad for Sidney. No wonder you two were freaking out so hard. I bet Buck is going to be grounded for eternity."

"Yeah. Probably." At least we don't have to call off the engagement.

* * * *

"How's Violet?"

"She's already in bed. She was exhausted."

"I bet."

Sidney ushers me inside the house and I follow him through the kitchen, which has been cleaned, to the backyard, which I'm also assuming has been cleaned since there are no red cups littering the lawn. "How's Buck? I mean, Miller." Violet is now insisting she call Miller by his nickname rather than his given name.

"He's banished to his room with no TV and no devices until the end of time. He cried when Violet texted. He really couldn't remember what happened."

I press my hand to my chest. "It's sweet that he cried, but scary that he couldn't remember."

"Hence, his being grounded for life." Sidney's gaze drops to my bare ring finger.

"It's in my nightstand drawer. I figured we should probably let the dust settle before we go sharing the news."

"That's a good idea. He was really worried that he'd messed things up. So was I, to be honest. I can't tell you how relieved I was when Violet texted."

"I cried loudly in a fast-food parking lot, then relief binged on burgers and fries."

"That sounds like a reasonable thing to do." He wraps his arms around me. "Lesson learned, huh? Miller will stay with his grandparents when I go away, since I can't trust him on his own."

"How does he feel about that?"

"He knows he has to earn my trust back after this."

Sidney releases me when there's a knock on the sliding glass door. I turn to find Miller standing on the other side, looking a lot like a sad golden retriever. His big shoulders are hunched, one of his thumbs is tucked into his shorts pocket and his bottom lip slips through his teeth.

Sidney motions for him to open the door.

"Sorry to interrupt, but I saw Skye's car in the driveway. I can come back later, though. Or maybe you don't really want to talk to me right now." He drops his head and stares at his feet.

I glance at Sidney. "It's okay. Is there something you want to say, Miller?"

He nods and rubs the back of his neck. "I uh...my dad really likes you. Like a lot. And I like you a lot, too. And I know I fu—messed up this weekend. And that Violet is only sixteen and what I did was stupid and dangerous. Especially because I got hammered and then she had to be the one to take care of me instead of the other way around. And that's not to say she can't take care of herself. But all my friends were here, and she doesn't know them and some of them can be real douchebags, but I don't think they were douchebags to her." He sucks in a long breath. "Anyway, I wanted to say that I'm sorry. And I promise to do better. I've never had the chance to be an older brother, but I think Violet would be a great sister, even if we're both almost adults and I'm probably going to be on a farm team in a year. So, yeah. I'm sorry and it won't happen again, and not just because I'm grounded until I move out."

"It wasn't your best choice, but you're a teenage boy, and your kind aren't known for making the best, rational decisions. I forgive you."

His head snaps up, his eyes wide with surprise. "You do?"

"It can't ever happen again."

"It won't. I promise."

"I'll wax your arms and legs if it does."

He rubs the fuzz on his forearm. "That's a fair and just punishment."

I open my arms. "Want a hug?"

He nods and engulfs me in his enormous arms. He smells like body spray, sweat and dirty socks. "Thanks for being so cool, Skye."

"It's easier for me since I'm not the one who has to dole out or enforce the punishment. Remember this moment when you feel like giving your dad a hard time about it?"

"You should go to bed, son. You have a busy day and practice tomorrow after school," Sidney says.

"Okay. Good night. And tell Vi I'm sorry again. And thanks for making sure I didn't die like an asshole."

"Will do."

Miller disappears back inside and trudges upstairs to his bedroom.

"I think when you're ready, we can probably tell them?"

Sidney's eyes light up. "Yeah?"

"Yeah. I think Violet already suspects something, anyway."

"How about a barbecue later this week?"

"That would be perfect."

Chapter Twenty-Two

I Called It

Violet

Intuition tells me that something big is about to happen. Well, it's less about intuition and more about observation. My mother has spent an inordinate amount of time disappearing into her bedroom since she came back from her weekend away with Sidney. She's never gone for long, just a few minutes, but when she returns, she's always sporting a dreamy smile.

At first I thought maybe she was taking care of personal business, which isn't something any sixteen-year-old girl wants to consider too carefully when it comes to her mom. We're pretty open, but there are some lines that should never be crossed. It was happening so frequently, though, I decided that couldn't possibly be it.

And then comes the mid-week barbecue at Sidney's. That isn't too unusual considering it's summer and the nice weather only lasts so long in Chicago, so we definitely want to take advantage of it while we can. But add in the incessant text messages, phone calls where she disappears for several minutes because apparently the content requires privacy, and then when she returns, she's all squirrelly and nervous.

"Do you have your lactose pills?" she asks for the tenth time.

"Yes mom, I have my lactose pills."

"And your bathing suit?" She rummages around in her purse for the seven hundred and fifty-second time in the past ten minutes.

I hold up the giant beach bag that contains not only my bathing suit, but my favorite towel, a romance book in case listening to Buck talk about hockey gets boring and I need to tune him out, a change of clothes and a lot of sunblock. "Yup."

"So you're ready to go?" She's still digging around in her purse.

"Yes, mom. I'm ready to go. Are you making a stop in Narnia first, or channeling your inner Mary Poppins?"

"Huh?" She stops her purse rummaging to look at me.

I prop a fist on my hip and arch a brow. "You're basically trying to climb into your purse. What's going on? What are you looking for?"

She blinks at me for several long seconds. "I'm just making sure I have everything I need."

I drop it. For now. This is what she does when we travel; compulsively checks her purse for her driver's license, even though she always keeps it in her wallet. It doesn't matter if it was there two minutes ago, she'll still check again, like an inanimate card is going to sprout a pair of legs and walk off.

We hop into the car and drive over to Sidney's. Mom is antsy as hell. Neither of us is awesome at keeping secrets or hiding things from each other, so I'm about ten thousand percent sure one of two things is going to happen today. She asks me the same three questions twice. I don't call her on it.

Sidney is already on the front porch when we arrive. Another sure sign something is going down.

"Hi, Violet. Miller's out back by the pool if you want to join him. I'll help your mom bring everything in." Sidney pats me on the shoulder.

"Sure. Sounds good." A couple of minutes alone with Buck is exactly what I need. He's been messaging relentlessly since the weekend, making sure we're still cool. I have a feeling he remembers bits and pieces of our conversation before he tossed his cookies.

If I'm right about what I think is coming today, it will serve me well to have something to hold over Buck in the future. Just in case he gets it in his head to throw another party with his hockey buddies when our parents inevitably go away again.

I find Buck skimming leaves out of the pool. It seems to be one of his favorite pastimes.

"Vi! Hey. Hi." His eyes go wide and his gaze shifts behind me. "Where are the 'rents?"

"Inside, doing whatever."

He puts the net back and rushes over. "I'm so sorry about Saturday night. Thanks for not letting me die. And whatever I said, I didn't mean it. Unless it was an apology. I meant those."

"Do you mean the part about me being forbidden fruit?" I arch a brow.

His eyes widen further. "Oh God. I said that. I hoped it was all in my head. I didn't mean it the way it came out. However, it came out."

"I'm sure you didn't." Is it awful that I'm allowing him to believe he made an actual pass at me? Probably. But if our parents end up getting married, I'll be his younger stepsister. His douchebag friends might decide to torment me because I'm a certified nerd and I'm horrifyingly clumsy. But if I have something to hold over his head, he'll be compelled to defend me. Even though Buck makes some questionable choices, and he seems like he's on the path to becoming a player, he's a genuinely nice guy. He'll feel bad about this for as long as I allow him to believe it's true. Which may or may not be forever.

"You won't tell my dad, will you?" He looks like he's about to pee his swim trunks.

"It's never going to happen again, is it?"

He shakes his head vehemently. "No. God no. I was wasted and talking out of my ass. I don't look at you like that. I'm kinda hoping you're going to be my sister. Stepsister. But still. We'll be related one day. Maybe." He stares at me for a few long seconds. I'm not sure what he's waiting for. "I have like five hundred dollars in cash in my room. You can have it."

I tip my head. "Like hush money?"

"Yes. No. You made sure I didn't die, even after I said whatever I said. And you're not gonna tell my dad. You should have seen him on Sunday. He was so mad at me. So damn mad. And I was scared your mom was going to break up with him. I haven't had a mom since before I really remember what having a mom is like. And Skye is such a cool lady. And fun. And I get that I'm like, almost eighteen and stuff, but I don't want to do anything that might mess up the chance that she might become my stepmom. God, I hope I'm not jinxing this whole thing."

My heart squeezes and my empathy buttons start firing. Not enough for me to tell him the full story of Saturday night, but enough to assuage his fears. "I get what you mean. My grandparents have been like a second set of parents all my life, but I've never had a dad. I don't even actually know who my real dad is. But it's been nice seeing my mom so happy, and it'd be cool to have an older brother, even if the only thing we really have in common is that we're both teenagers."

He blinks twice, like he's trying to decode the underlying message.

"I don't need hush money. Just don't let your hockey buddies bully me, and we're good. And I might need the occasional drive somewhere, and if you play professional hockey and you're making the big bucks, I'm not against you picking up the tab for my milkshake and fries obsession when you're in town."

"Deal."

We shake on it. His palms are sweaty so we both wipe them on our shorts after.

Our parents come out. Sidney is carrying a tray of appetizers and mom is clasping her hands together, wearing a really weird smile.

"Snack time!" Mom's voice is all high and pitchy.

"I'll grab drinks!" Buck offers.

"I can help." I follow him into the pool house. "Something is going on today. My mom is acting strange. Stranger than usual, even."

"My dad has been the same for the past couple of days. He's been all smiles since Skye came over Sunday night. Usually, when I've done something stupid and irresponsible, he's grumpy for a couple of days, but it hasn't been the case this time around."

"Huh. Well, I feel like they're gearing up for the big reveal of whatever it is." Buck passes me a bottle of white wine and a grape soda, then grabs a beer and an orange soda for himself. He doesn't spike it with vodka this time.

Sidney and Mom are sitting at the outdoor dining table, the appetizer platter set in the middle. Mom's hands are folded together, and she's still wearing that creepy, weird smile that looks like it belongs on one of those awful dolls with the eyes that blink. I give her a questioning look, but all she does is continue to grin.

Buck passes his dad the beer and pops the cork on the wine bottle, then pours half of it into a stemless wine glass for my mom. She murmurs a thank you and takes a seriously hefty gulp.

"All right. What's going on?" I cross my arms. "Mom, you've got your creepy smile thing going on. Someone needs to spill the beans, whatever the beans are."

Mom and Sidney look at each other. "We have some news we'd like to share."

"Oh shit! Skye's preggers, isn't she!" Buck holds his hand up to his dad for a high five. "Your swimmers still work!"

Sidney stares at Buck's outstretched hand.

I knock it out of the air. "My mom isn't preggers. She's drinking a bowl of wine. You can't drink when you're pregnant and she has an IUD."

"What does drinking and driving have to do with getting pregnant? Unless those things all happened at the same time," Buck's eyes go wide.

"Not a DUI, an IUD, intrauterine device. It's a form of birth control," I explain.

"Oh. Well, that makes a lot more sense. So no one is pregnant?" Buck looks from me to my mom and back to me, eyes widening again.

"I've never even made it past second base with anyone but myself, so no, no one is pregnant."

Sidney coughs.

Mom thrusts her hand out like this is some kind of sports circle where they all put their hand in the middle and do the whole "we're going to kick some ass" thing. Buck clearly thinks this is what's happening because his hand shoots out too.

But before his giant of a mitt covers hers, I spot the massive rock decorating her finger. I slap Buck's hand away and grab my mom's wrist. In the process I knock over my chair and my grape soda, which, by some miracle, Buck catches before it makes a mess.

"Oh my God! That's an engagement ring! You got engaged? You're getting married? Fuck! I should have put money on this! I knew something big was going down!" I shout.

I release my mom's hand and trip over the leg of the chair as I try to round the table. I go sprawling across the patio, scraping both of my palms and my right knee and my glasses go flying.

Buck, being the ridiculously agile and not-clumsy soon-to-be-stepbrother that he is, picks me up and sets me on my feet, then hands me my glasses.

"Thanks. I wish my feet were better at their job."

Sidney, being the smart, thoughtful guy he is, quickly stands and pulls my mom's chair out for her so she doesn't suffer the same fate. We both step to the edge of the table, throw our hands in the air, and scream obnoxiously loud.

"You're getting hitched!" I shout.

"I am!" she shouts back.

We rush each other, our boobs slamming together, causing us to grunt in discomfort, but we wrap our arms around each other and hug and jump up and down until we step on each other's feet. Then we just sway back and forth.

"You're okay with this?" Mom whispers.

"More than okay." I squeeze her tight.

It's been the two of us for a damn long time. We're ready to add some testosterone to the estrogen fest.

Buck and Sid are standing side by side, wearing matching smiles. Buck looks like maybe he's on the edge of getting emotional. Dude is a huge freaking fuzzy yeti-bear.

Mom gives him a questioning smile and opens her arms. He takes the invitation and folds her in a hug. "Pretty damn excited that you're gonna be my mom." He opens his arms. "Family hug!"

Sid and I join, and I end up with my face mashed into Buck's sweaty armpit for a second before we shuffle around and it turns into more of a huddle.

It's awkward and silly and exactly what I always wanted for us.

Epilogue

The Big Day

Skye

Nine months later

"You look amazing, mom." Violet pulls a tissue from between her boobs and dabs under her eyes, then tucks it back in her bra.

I take her hands in mine and squeeze. "So do you. God, I'm nervous. I feel like this dress is a little on the flashy side." Because it's my first time down the aisle, Sidney wanted our special day to be a lavish affair. Even my dressing room is like something straight out of a fairytale. Except for my dress. It's probably more appropriate for Vegas, but it's too late to turn back now.

"It's perfect. Your boobs look great, and Sidney's going to lose his mind when he sees you. What do you need? How can I help?"

"Just a hug would be great right about now. You look stunning. All grown up." I pull her in for a boob smashing hug then step back. "Are you wearing heels?"

"Yeah. But I have flip-flops for the reception. I practiced walking in the hallway, so I'm reasonably confident that I'll make it down the aisle without falling flat on my face." She holds up her crossed fingers. Her clutch dangles from her wrist. "Oh! I have something for you. It's your something new. It's kind of inappropriate and also kind of hilarious. I'll completely understand if you don't want to wear it, or if you want to keep it as memento or never to show it to anyone else. Totally up to you." She pulls a small velvet drawstring bag out of her purse and thrusts it at me.

I open the delicate bag and fish out the item. It's a garter. But it's not the usual lace and satin business. It's definitely a Violet design. My daughter might be a math nerd, but she's a wizard with a sewing machine. "Oh my God, where did you find penis fabric?"

"At the fabric store. Surprisingly, it was on clearance. Like I said, you don't have to wear it. Maybe Sid will want to hang it from his rearview mirror. Or not."

"You're my favorite person in the entire world. I'm not tossing this during the reception. I'm keeping it forever." I hug it to my chest.

My mother knocks on the door and pokes her head inside. "Oh sweetheart, you look so beautiful. You too, Vi. Everyone ready? It's almost showtime!" She claps. "Is it okay if your dad comes in?"

"Absolutely."

"Herman, you're allowed in." Mom tosses over her shoulder.

My dad joins us in the bridal room and gets all misty eyed, which makes me misty eyed and there's a lot of tipping our chins to the ceiling so we don't mess up our expensive makeup or end up with red eyes before I even walk down the aisle and drink too much champagne at the reception.

The wedding planner pops her head in and tells us it's go time. Violet and my mom give me hugs and leave the bridal suite ahead of us. I didn't want a hoard of bridesmaids to manage, so it's just my mom and Violet walking down the aisle before me.

"You ready, honey?" My dad links arms with me.

"More ready than I ever thought I'd be." My legs are a little wobbly as we follow mom and Violet out of the suite.

I'm hidden from view as I watch my mom walk down the aisle, followed by Violet. She only sort of stutter steps and lists to the right once. Miller, who is already standing at the front takes a hesitant step forward, as if he's going to meet her halfway, but she holds up a hand, squares her shoulders, grabs the hem of dress and hoists it up a few inches while muttering, "Freaking heels are a death trap."

A quiet chuckle moves through the attendees and my great Aunt Brenda says loud enough so that everyone can hear, "Men designed them!"

When Violet reaches the front of the church, everyone bursts into applause. Her face turns red.

I turn to my wedding planner. "Can you do me a solid and get Violet an antihistamine so she doesn't end up with a full-blown case of hives after this, please?"

"Already taken care of, she took one half an hour ago."

"Thank God." The wedding march cues up.

Dad pats my arm. "All right sweetheart, let's get you hitched."

"Let's do this." I take a deep breath and we round the corner, bringing Sidney and all our friends and family into view.

Everyone stands, but my eyes stay locked on the hot as hell man waiting for me at the end of the aisle. "Oh wow," I mutter. "He cleans up nice."

Dad squeezes my arm. "Inside voice, Skye. Everyone can hear you."

I shrug. "Looking good, babe!" I call down the aisle.

Sidney's grin widens as his eyes move over me in a not so PG-13 sweep. Tonight, we're definitely going to swing from the rafters.

My dad has to slow me down because I try to speed walk down the aisle to Sidney, but eventually, after what feels like a million years, my dad kisses my cheek and passes me off to my husband to be.

"You look darn well edible," I whisper as Sidney takes my hands.

"So do you."

"I can't wait to get you o—"

Sidney stops me with a brief, chaste kiss. "Audience, babe."

"Right. Save it for later." I back off and wave to our friends and family. "Hi, sorry about that. He looks good, though, right?"

"I wouldn't kick him out of bed," Aunt Brenda shouts.

Sidney looks like he's trying not to laugh.

Our officiant looks like she expected exactly this, which makes sense since Aunt Brenda came to the run-through two days ago and ad-libbed the entire time.

The ceremony begins with the usual stuff, the officiant talking about joining lives and all that jazz and then it's time for Sid and me to say our vows. Which we wrote ourselves.

"Skye, I've waited a long time to find someone who balances me out. You're everything I need in a partner and more. You're so full of life, you keep me on my toes, and you make me smile every day. I love everything about you, from your unfiltered thoughts, to the way you champion Violet and the way you've stepped in and become the mom Miller needs. I promise to stand by your side through the good times and especially the bad, to be your partner and your rock when you need me the most. You're my best friend, and I can't wait to spend the rest of my life loving you."

I pull a tissue from between my boobs and dab my eyes. "That's going to be a tough one to follow."

He squeezes my hands. "You got this."

Violet moves forward and hands me my cue card, and nearly trips over the back of her dress when she steps back. We both blow out a relieved breath when she finds her balance.

I turn back to Sidney and hold up the card. "Made a few notes in case my mind goes blank and I forget all the awesome things I wrote about you."

He smiles and squeezes my hand. I glance at the cue card, skim the first few points and then refocus on him. "When you chased after me and stopped me from drinking your latte, I already knew you were one of the good ones. Although, you didn't learn until later just how thoroughly you'd saved my a—butt that day. What I didn't realize was that you were exactly what I needed in my life and you came into it at exactly the right time. You are an incredible father, an amazing scout and coach, an unparalleled friend, and the only time I'll kick you out of bed is if you're snoring like a freight train lives inside your nasal passage. I promise to stand beside you through all the fun stuff, and hold your hand through the hard times. I love everything about who you are on the inside and the outside. Your hair is particularly fantastic and I can't wait to run my fingers through it later. After the reception."

"Mom, stay on track," Violet whispers.

"Right. Sorry." I squeeze Sid's hand. "I love you. You're the best thing to happen to me since Violet came into my life and I can't wait to spend the rest of it with you."

I blow out a breath, thankful I didn't say anything too awkward and then we're exchanging rings and saying "I do".

"You may kiss the bride!" our officiant announces.

Sidney lays one on me.

"Save it for the honeymoon!" Aunt Brenda shouts.

We walk down the aisle, waving at our friends as they clap and holler.

The next few hours are a blur of photos, champagne, congratulations and one kid throwing up because he ate too many cookies.

Dinner is amazing, the wine is flowing, everyone is half-sauced, and it's time for the speeches. Miller gets up, adjusts his tie and pulls Violet's chair out.

I put my hand on Sidney's knee under the table. "I didn't know Violet was giving a speech."

"I think Miller is mostly talking," he assures me.

Violet switched from heels to flip-flops when we arrived at the hall for the reception. She focuses on her feet as she walks the twenty feet across the raised platform. I glance at her empty spot and notice there's a mostly empty glass of wine beside her plate.

Miller keeps one hand poised behind her as if he's ready to catch her should she stumble. A little kid screams about ice cream from the guest tables. Miller glances toward the audience as Violet takes the first step down, and then everything goes terribly sideways.

And it's all being broadcast on the big screen on the other side of the hall. Violet's dress gets caught between her flip flop and her heel and the whole bodice slides down. Miller gazelle-leaps off the stage while simultaneously shrugging out of his suit jacket. He quickly drapes it over Violet, but it's too late, everyone has already seen her tatas.

The entire room goes pin-drop silent.

I push my chair back and hop to my feet. Sidney moves to stand, but I put a hand on his shoulder. "I got this." I quickly strut across the raised platform, pausing at Violet's spot to grab her clutch and rush to help.

I make eye contact with Aunt Brenda and she gives me a curt nod, and then opens her duffle bag sized purse and starts handing out a round of Jell-O shooters. If ever there was a time to get our guests as sauced as possible, it's now.

Miller's eyes are as wide as saucers and Violet is the color of a ripe tomato. He's holding his suit jacket up like a shield. Violet's back is facing the guests and thankfully the videographer has shifted his focus. Unfortunately, he's panning across the stricken faces of the guests. Everyone has seen my daughter's boobs. This one is going to be hard to live down.

Violet looks like she's about to burst into tears. "Cover us so I can get her to the bathroom," I tell Miller.

He nods, eyes still wide, and not blinking. He follows us to the door and I wrap a protective arm around Violet, ushering her into the bridal suite and locking the door behind us.

"Oh my God." She blinks at me. "Everyone saw my boobs. The flip-flops were supposed to prevent a wardrobe malfunction, not cause one!" She flails her arms around like the inflatable balloon guy on a particularly windy day.

"Everyone is drunk on wine and the vodka Jell-O shooters Aunt Brenda brought along in her picnic basket." She was handing them out just before the reception.

"Is that why they burned going down? I think she was giving them to the little kids, too." Violet blows out a breath. "Remind me to never wear a strapless dress ever again. I thought the double-sided tape was going to be enough to keep it in place, but obviously I was wrong. Buck saw my boobs. Up close and personal. It's going to be awkward now forever."

"It's only awkward if you make it awkward."

Violet gives me a pinched, disbelieving look.

"Okay. It'll be a little awkward, but let's look on the bright side of things. You have a great rack. Your boobs still hold themselves up, if ever there was a time to have a wardrobe malfunction, it's now, when they're perky and gravity hasn't dragged the bitches down to your knees and you don't need enough under-wire to build an entire birdcage with." I motion to my own girls, strapped into an under-wire prison so they sit high and mighty on my chest.

"I'm never getting married. I should have let Buck go up on his own, but I wanted to be moral support in case his cue cards gave him a hard time and now my boobs have been seen by like a thousand people."

"There are only seventy guests, Violet."

"I'm being extra because I flashed everyone! If I get married one day, I'm eloping. Maybe to an island, or maybe not because I feel like I'd get sand in my underwear and it would suck, or I'd fall into the ocean. Maybe Vegas would be better."

I grab my daughter by the shoulders. "You can get married wherever you want. Everyone is drunk, honey. Speeches are boring and no one pays attention to them, anyway. Aunt Brenda is handing out more shooters, and she probably used her own moonshine in them, so they're super potent. No one will remember this even happened. And Miller was quick to cover you up."

She bites her lips together and sighs. "He's an annoyingly good stepbrother."

"He's doing a solid job so far." I rub her shoulders. "Want to chug a glass of champagne before we go back out there?"

"Seems like a good idea, but maybe before you do that, we can put on these invisible bra straps so I don't have another accident. She digs them out of the pocket in her dress.

"Good plan."

We strap her boobs in and then each down a glass of champagne.

"Ready to go back out there? Speeches should almost be over."

"Yeah, I'm ready."

I take her back out to the reception. Miller has already finished his speech. He hops up and meets us, taking Vi's hand as she carefully climbs the stairs, and Sidney and I take our place behind the podium. I drag his mouth down to mine and make a spectacle while Miller walks Violet back to her seat to keep the attention off her and it works.

I let Sidney take the reins on our speech, mostly because that champagne has gone right to my head and then the DJ cues the first dance.

"Is Violet okay?" Sidney asks as we move around the dance floor.

"She'll be fine. Eventually. When the embarrassment wears off." I glance over to find Miller with his arms crossed, glaring at the male server who has suddenly taken an interest in my daughter. "Awww, look, he's being her bodyguard. They're just like real siblings."

"He's really settling into the big brother role," Sidney agrees.

I smile up at him and he dips down to kiss me.

Everything feels like it's clicking into place. I have a fabulous daughter, a stepson who has her back, and now a husband who's my best friend and a total freak in the sheets.

Life is perfect, and it's just the beginning.

Sign up for the 1001 Dark Nights Newsletter
and be entered to win a Tiffany Key necklace.

There's a contest every month!

Go to www.1001DarkNights.com to subscribe.

**As a bonus, all subscribers can download
FIVE FREE exclusive books!**

Discover 1001 Dark Nights Collection Ten

DRAGON LOVER by Donna Grant
A Dragon Kings Novella

KEEPING YOU by Aurora Rose Reynolds
An Until Him/Her Novella

HAPPILY EVER NEVER by Carrie Ann Ryan
A Montgomery Ink Legacy Novella

DESTINED FOR ME by Corinne Michaels
A Come Back for Me/Say You'll Stay Crossover

MADAM ALANA by Audrey Carlan
A Marriage Auction Novella

DIRTY FILTHY BILLIONAIRE by Laurelin Paige
A Dirty Universe Novella

HIDE AND SEEK by Laura Kaye
A Blasphemy Novella

TANGLED WITH YOU by J. Kenner
A Stark Security Novella

TEMPTED by Lexi Blake
A Masters and Mercenaries Novella

THE DANDELION DIARY by Devney Perry
A Maysen Jar Novella

CHERRY LANE by Kristen Proby
A Huckleberry Bay Novella

THE GRAVE ROBBER by Darynda Jones
A Charley Davidson Novella

CRY OF THE BANSHEE by Heather Graham
A Krewe of Hunters Novella

DARKEST NEED by Rachel Van Dyken
A Dark Ones Novella

CHRISTMAS IN CAPE MAY by Jennifer Probst
A Sunshine Sisters Novella

A VAMPIRE'S MATE by Rebecca Zanetti
A Dark Protectors/Rebels Novella

WHERE IT BEGINS by Helena Hunting
A Pucked Novella

Also from Blue Box Press

THE MARRIAGE AUCTION by Audrey Carlan
Book One
Book Two
Book Three
Book Four

THE JEWELER OF STOLEN DREAMS by M.J. Rose

SAPPHIRE STORM by Christopher Rice writing as C. Travis Rice
A Sapphire Cove Novel

ATLAS: THE STORY OF PA SALT by Lucinda Riley and Harry Whittaker

A SOUL OF ASH AND BLOOD by Jennifer L. Armentrout
A Blood and Ash Novel

START US UP by Lexi Blake
A Park Avenue Promise Novel

LOVE ON THE BYLINE by Xio Axelrod
A Plays and Players Novel

FIGHTING THE PULL by Kristen Ashley
A River Rain Novel

A FIRE IN THE FLESH by Jennifer L. Armentrout
A Flesh and Fire Novel

Pucked

By Helena Hunting
The Pucked Series, Book One

The 1st standalone novel in The Pucked Series

With a famous NHL player for a stepbrother, Violet Hall is well acquainted with the playboy reputation of many a hockey star. So of course she isn't interested in legendary team captain Alex Waters or his pretty, beat-up face and rock-hard six-pack abs. When Alex inadvertently obliterates Violet's misapprehension regarding the inferior intellect of hockey players, he becomes much more than just a hot body with the face to match.

Suffering from a complete lapse in judgment, Violet discovers just how good Alex is with the hockey stick in his pants. Violet believes her night of orgasmic magic with Alex is just that: one night. But Alex starts to call. And text. And email and send extravagant—and quirky—gifts. Suddenly, he's too difficult to ignore, and nearly impossible not to like.

The problem is, the media portrays Alex as a total player, and Violet doesn't want to be part of the game.

* * * *

Excerpt:

It's 6:51 on Thursday morning, and I'm thirty seconds away from an amazing orgasm. Women everywhere should take a page from the man manual. Just because I don't sport the obvious signs men do, such as morning wood, doesn't mean I shouldn't take care of my personal needs before I hit the shower. My day is always better when I start with a shot from the orgasm bottle.

I'm right there, teetering on the brink of heaven. Every nerve ending is on fire in the best way possible. My muscles are tight, fingers moving at a furious pace, the vibrator—God bless the damn vibrator—is hitting the s-s-s-spot, and everything is about to go blissfully white.

And that's the moment my mother's shrill voice breaks all orgasmic magic, destroying my morning jill-off. She must have let herself in again, as is typical.

Here's the thing; I don't live with my mom. I moved out more than four years ago—into the damn pool house. Technically, it's on the same piece of property, but it's supposed to be my private space. My refuge from my crazy awesome, albeit super-inappropriate mother.

The door to my bedroom crashes open as I shut off the vibe and pull up the covers. My vagina is raging. I can't even begin to explain. It's the female equivalent of blue balls.

"Mom!" I slump further under the comforter. "How many times do we need to have this talk?"

"You should be out of bed already! I have something for you!" She waves her hands around in the air like the crazy inflatable balloon guy on TV. It's too much this early in my day.

"I literally just woke up. I need five minutes before we have a conversation, okay?"

Her arms fall to her sides, her shoulders dropping with her smile, which would make me feel bad, except she's let herself into my home and barged into my bedroom unannounced. So all I have is frustration.

"Oh, sure." Her dejection is blissfully short-lived. "How about I put on a pot of coffee?"

My mom loves to be useful, and while I'm annoyed, I don't want to hurt her feelings in spite of the inconvenient interruption. "That'd be great." Any reason to get her out of my room is a good one, but a fresh pot of coffee is more than welcome.

She backs out and closes the door, leaving me in peace. For three seconds I contemplate finishing what I started, but there's no way I'm going to come with my mom tooling around in my kitchen. Instead, I toss my vibe into the nightstand and make a stop in the bathroom to wash my hands.

At twenty-two, I should be able to maintain some distance from my mother. However, she has a great deal of difficulty with the concept of personal space. In my freshman year of college, I threw out the idea of moving into an apartment close to campus. My mom and Sidney—my stepdad—had recently tied the knot. They were worse than virginal teenagers. I've had the misfortune of walking in on them in compromising positions more than once. The third time was my breaking point.

Guilt-ridden and embarrassed by the psychological damage he had caused, Sidney offered to renovate the pool house. I agreed only because it saved me thousands on rent.

When I first scored my job several months ago, I started looking for my own apartment again, in part because of the frequency of my mother's unplanned visits. Being the ever helpful parent, she tagged along on the expedition and told me roommate horror stories à la Single White Female. Seeing as the only places I could reasonably afford were shared accommodations, I chose to stay put in the pool house a while longer. As I no longer carry the burden of tuition, revisiting that option seems like a good plan.

I wipe my vagina-scent-free hands on my T-shirt as I enter the kitchen. My mom sits at the table and leafs through one of the gossip rags she loves to read while she sips a cup of coffee.

"I think they made Buck look way worse here than he really is, don't you?" She turns the magazine around so I can see the horrible pictures of my stepbrother.

I grab a mug, fill it with liquid heaven, and drop into the chair across from my mom. "I think Buck does a decent job of making himself look bad all on his own without the help of the media."

My stepbrother is such a whore. I'm tempted to apply this label to all professional hockey players. It's a blanket statement, an overzealous and possibly incorrect generalization. However, based on personal experience, I believe it's true for the most part. It certainly applies to the one hockey player I dated last year. I consider him to be like Voldemort: he who shall not be named.

The third page of last week's entertainment section confirms this hypothesis. The evidence is splashed all over the grainy two-page spread of Buck with his hand up some woman's skirt. In a public bathroom. He appears to be devouring her face while getting her naked inside a stall—with the door open. So dirty.

The picture itself isn't a surprise. Hundreds of similar images can be found through an Internet search. Buck has shared his manstick with half the female population in the continental US, and probably a few up in Canada. The woman he's making out with is the problem. He's not macking on a random hockey hooker. Oh no. It's his former coach's niece. Her name is Fran. She's adorable, and now she looks like a total puck bunny, thanks to Buck.

In his defense, he said he didn't know who she was. He's not bright and he was hammered, so it likely was an honest mistake—not that it makes his whoring ways any less abhorrent. This little incident is the reason behind his recent trade. His return to Chicago means I'll be seeing a lot more of him again.

"Well, I think they've blown this way out of proportion. Sidney's excited to have him back in the city, though. Anyway..." She pushes a piece of paper toward me. Upon inspection, I realize it's a plane ticket.

I snatch it up and frown. "What's this? Why does it have my name on it? What's in Atlanta?"

"Surprise!" She does jazz hands. "It's Buck's first away game."

"Mom, I can't—"

"We're going as a family to support him. He's had a rough couple of weeks."

"It's not my fault Buck can't keep his dick in his pants and out of his coach's niece."

"Violet!" Her brow arches and her lips purse as if she's sucking a lemon. "Don't be so crass! This isn't about Buck's..." She trails off and gestures below the table.

"Yes it is. Buck doesn't care if I come to his games."

"He was very upset when you couldn't make the last few. Maybe if you'd been at this one"—she points at the magazine—"he might not have gotten himself into so much trouble."

"Are you guilting me into coming?" I glare over the rim of my mug.

"Not at all. I'm just throwing out hypotesticals."

I cough-choke. "Do you mean hypotheticals?"

"That's what I said."

Correcting her is as pointless as fighting her on this. Once my mom makes up her mind, rationalizing an alternative is like slamming your head into a titanium wall—painful and futile. I need to reconsider the apartment situation.

I give getting out of going to the game a last-ditch effort. "I have to work this weekend."

"No you don't."

"How do you know?"

She ignores the question. "A car will be at the house to pick us up at six."

"I don't get off until five. How are we even going to make it to the game on time?"

"The flight isn't until tomorrow morning." She taps the date on the ticket, which I've failed to read.

"Oh." So much for finding a way out. It looks like I'm going to another hockey game. Yippee.

About Helena Hunting

NYT and *USA Today* bestselling author, Helena Hunting, lives on the outskirts of Toronto with her incredibly tolerant family and two moderately intolerant cats. She writes contemporary romance and romantic comedies, and when she wants to dive into her angsty side, she writes new adult romance under H. Hunting.

Visit helenahunting.com for more information.

Discover 1001 Dark Nights

COLLECTION ONE
FOREVER WICKED by Shayla Black ~ CRIMSON TWILIGHT by Heather Graham ~ CAPTURED IN SURRENDER by Liliana Hart ~ SILENT BITE: A SCANGUARDS WEDDING by Tina Folsom ~ DUNGEON GAMES by Lexi Blake ~ AZAGOTH by Larissa Ione ~ NEED YOU NOW by Lisa Renee Jones ~ SHOW ME, BABY by Cherise Sinclair~ ROPED IN by Lorelei James ~ TEMPTED BY MIDNIGHT by Lara Adrian ~ THE FLAME by Christopher Rice ~ CARESS OF DARKNESS by Julie Kenner

COLLECTION TWO
WICKED WOLF by Carrie Ann Ryan ~ WHEN IRISH EYES ARE HAUNTING by Heather Graham ~ EASY WITH YOU by Kristen Proby ~ MASTER OF FREEDOM by Cherise Sinclair ~ CARESS OF PLEASURE by Julie Kenner ~ ADORED by Lexi Blake ~ HADES by Larissa Ione ~ RAVAGED by Elisabeth Naughton ~ DREAM OF YOU by Jennifer L. Armentrout ~ STRIPPED DOWN by Lorelei James ~ RAGE/KILLIAN by Alexandra Ivy/Laura Wright ~ DRAGON KING by Donna Grant ~ PURE WICKED by Shayla Black ~ HARD AS STEEL by Laura Kaye ~ STROKE OF MIDNIGHT by Lara Adrian ~ ALL HALLOWS EVE by Heather Graham ~ KISS THE FLAME by Christopher Rice~ DARING HER LOVE by Melissa Foster ~ TEASED by Rebecca Zanetti ~ THE PROMISE OF SURRENDER by Liliana Hart

COLLECTION THREE
HIDDEN INK by Carrie Ann Ryan ~ BLOOD ON THE BAYOU by Heather Graham ~ SEARCHING FOR MINE by Jennifer Probst ~ DANCE OF DESIRE by Christopher Rice ~ ROUGH RHYTHM by Tessa Bailey ~ DEVOTED by Lexi Blake ~ Z by Larissa Ione ~ FALLING UNDER YOU by Laurelin Paige ~ EASY FOR KEEPS by Kristen Proby ~ UNCHAINED by Elisabeth Naughton ~ HARD TO SERVE by Laura Kaye ~ DRAGON FEVER by Donna Grant ~ KAYDEN/SIMON by Alexandra Ivy/Laura Wright ~ STRUNG UP by Lorelei James ~ MIDNIGHT UNTAMED by Lara Adrian ~ TRICKED by Rebecca Zanetti ~ DIRTY WICKED by Shayla Black ~

THE ONLY ONE by Lauren Blakely ~ SWEET SURRENDER by Liliana Hart

COLLECTION FOUR

ROCK CHICK REAWAKENING by Kristen Ashley ~ ADORING INK by Carrie Ann Ryan ~ SWEET RIVALRY by K. Bromberg ~ SHADE'S LADY by Joanna Wylde ~ RAZR by Larissa Ione ~ ARRANGED by Lexi Blake ~ TANGLED by Rebecca Zanetti ~ HOLD ME by J. Kenner ~ SOMEHOW, SOME WAY by Jennifer Probst ~ TOO CLOSE TO CALL by Tessa Bailey ~ HUNTED by Elisabeth Naughton ~ EYES ON YOU by Laura Kaye ~ BLADE by Alexandra Ivy/Laura Wright ~ DRAGON BURN by Donna Grant ~ TRIPPED OUT by Lorelei James ~ STUD FINDER by Lauren Blakely ~ MIDNIGHT UNLEASHED by Lara Adrian ~ HALLOW BE THE HAUNT by Heather Graham ~ DIRTY FILTHY FIX by Laurelin Paige ~ THE BED MATE by Kendall Ryan ~ NIGHT GAMES by CD Reiss ~ NO RESERVATIONS by Kristen Proby ~ DAWN OF SURRENDER by Liliana Hart

COLLECTION FIVE

BLAZE ERUPTING by Rebecca Zanetti ~ ROUGH RIDE by Kristen Ashley ~ HAWKYN by Larissa Ione ~ RIDE DIRTY by Laura Kaye ~ ROME'S CHANCE by Joanna Wylde ~ THE MARRIAGE ARRANGEMENT by Jennifer Probst ~ SURRENDER by Elisabeth Naughton ~ INKED NIGHTS by Carrie Ann Ryan ~ ENVY by Rachel Van Dyken ~ PROTECTED by Lexi Blake ~ THE PRINCE by Jennifer L. Armentrout ~ PLEASE ME by J. Kenner ~ WOUND TIGHT by Lorelei James ~ STRONG by Kylie Scott ~ DRAGON NIGHT by Donna Grant ~ TEMPTING BROOKE by Kristen Proby ~ HAUNTED BE THE HOLIDAYS by Heather Graham ~ CONTROL by K. Bromberg ~ HUNKY HEARTBREAKER by Kendall Ryan ~ THE DARKEST CAPTIVE by Gena Showalter

COLLECTION SIX

DRAGON CLAIMED by Donna Grant ~ ASHES TO INK by Carrie Ann Ryan ~ ENSNARED by Elisabeth Naughton ~ EVERMORE by Corinne Michaels ~ VENGEANCE by Rebecca Zanetti ~ ELI'S TRIUMPH by Joanna Wylde ~ CIPHER by Larissa Ione ~ RESCUING MACIE by Susan Stoker ~ ENCHANTED by Lexi Blake ~ TAKE THE BRIDE by Carly Phillips ~ INDULGE ME by J.

Kenner ~ THE KING by Jennifer L. Armentrout ~ QUIET MAN by Kristen Ashley ~ ABANDON by Rachel Van Dyken ~ THE OPEN DOOR by Laurelin Paige ~ CLOSER by Kylie Scott ~ SOMETHING JUST LIKE THIS by Jennifer Probst ~ BLOOD NIGHT by Heather Graham ~ TWIST OF FATE by Jill Shalvis ~ MORE THAN PLEASURE YOU by Shayla Black ~ WONDER WITH ME by Kristen Proby ~ THE DARKEST ASSASSIN by Gena Showalter

COLLECTION SEVEN
THE BISHOP by Skye Warren ~ TAKEN WITH YOU by Carrie Ann Ryan ~ DRAGON LOST by Donna Grant ~ SEXY LOVE by Carly Phillips ~ PROVOKE by Rachel Van Dyken ~ RAFE by Sawyer Bennett ~ THE NAUGHTY PRINCESS by Claire Contreras ~ THE GRAVEYARD SHIFT by Darynda Jones ~ CHARMED by Lexi Blake ~ SACRIFICE OF DARKNESS by Alexandra Ivy ~ THE QUEEN by Jen Armentrout ~ BEGIN AGAIN by Jennifer Probst ~ VIXEN by Rebecca Zanetti ~ SLASH by Laurelin Paige ~ THE DEAD HEAT OF SUMMER by Heather Graham ~ WILD FIRE by Kristen Ashley ~ MORE THAN PROTECT YOU by Shayla Black ~ LOVE SONG by Kylie Scott ~ CHERISH ME by J. Kenner ~ SHINE WITH ME by Kristen Proby

COLLECTION EIGHT
DRAGON REVEALED by Donna Grant ~ CAPTURED IN INK by Carrie Ann Ryan ~ SECURING JANE by Susan Stoker ~ WILD WIND by Kristen Ashley ~ DARE TO TEASE by Carly Phillips ~ VAMPIRE by Rebecca Zanetti ~ MAFIA KING by Rachel Van Dyken ~ THE GRAVEDIGGER'S SON by Darynda Jones ~ FINALE by Skye Warren ~ MEMORIES OF YOU by J. Kenner ~ SLAYED BY DARKNESS by Alexandra Ivy ~ TREASURED by Lexi Blake ~ THE DAREDEVIL by Dylan Allen ~ BOND OF DESTINY by Larissa Ione ~ MORE THAN POSSESS YOU by Shayla Black ~ HAUNTED HOUSE by Heather Graham ~ MAN FOR ME by Laurelin Paige ~ THE RHYTHM METHOD by Kylie Scott ~ JONAH BENNETT by Tijan ~ CHANGE WITH ME by Kristen Proby ~ THE DARKEST DESTINY by Gena Showalter

COLLECTION NINE
DRAGON UNBOUND by Donna Grant ~ NOTHING BUT INK by

Carrie Ann Ryan ~ THE MASTERMIND by Dylan Allen ~ JUST ONE WISH by Carly Phillips ~ BEHIND CLOSED DOORS by Skye Warren ~ GOSSAMER IN THE DARKNESS by Kristen Ashley ~ THE CLOSE-UP by Kennedy Ryan ~ DELIGHTED by Lexi Blake ~ THE GRAVESIDE BAR AND GRILL by Darynda Jones ~ THE ANTI-FAN AND THE IDOL by Rachel Van Dyken ~ CHARMED BY YOU by J. Kenner ~ DESCEND TO DARKNESS by Heather Graham~ BOND OF PASSION by Larissa Ione ~ JUST WHAT I NEEDED by Kylie Scott

Discover Blue Box Press

TAME ME by J. Kenner ~ TEMPT ME by J. Kenner ~ DAMIEN by J. Kenner ~ TEASE ME by J. Kenner ~ REAPER by Larissa Ione ~ THE SURRENDER GATE by Christopher Rice ~ SERVICING THE TARGET by Cherise Sinclair ~ THE LAKE OF LEARNING by Steve Berry and M.J. Rose ~ THE MUSEUM OF MYSTERIES by Steve Berry and M.J. Rose ~ TEASE ME by J. Kenner ~ FROM BLOOD AND ASH by Jennifer L. Armentrout ~ QUEEN MOVE by Kennedy Ryan ~ THE HOUSE OF LONG AGO by Steve Berry and M.J. Rose ~ THE BUTTERFLY ROOM by Lucinda Riley ~ A KINGDOM OF FLESH AND FIRE by Jennifer L. Armentrout ~ THE LAST TIARA by M.J. Rose ~ THE CROWN OF GILDED BONES by Jennifer L. Armentrout ~ THE MISSING SISTER by Lucinda Riley ~ THE END OF FOREVER by Steve Berry and M.J. Rose ~ THE STEAL by C. W. Gortner and M.J. Rose ~ CHASING SERENITY by Kristen Ashley ~ A SHADOW IN THE EMBER by Jennifer L. Armentrout ~ THE BAIT by C.W. Gortner and M.J. Rose ~ THE FASHION ORPHANS by Randy Susan Meyers and M.J. Rose ~ TAKING THE LEAP by Kristen Ashley ~ SAPPHIRE SUNSET by Christopher Rice writing C. Travis Rice ~ THE WAR OF TWO QUEENS by Jennifer L. Armentrout ~ THE MURDERS AT FLEAT HOUSE by Lucinda Riley ~ THE HEIST by C.W. Gortner and M.J. Rose ~ SAPPHIRE SPRING by Christopher Rice writing as C. Travis Rice ~ MAKING THE MATCH by Kristen Ashley ~ A LIGHT IN THE FLAME by Jennifer L.

On Behalf of 1001 Dark Nights,
Liz Berry, M.J. Rose, and Jillian Stein would like to thank ~

Steve Berry
Doug Scofield
Benjamin Stein
Kim Guidroz
Chelle Olson
Tanaka Kangara
Asha Hossain
Chris Graham
Jessica Saunders
Stacey Tardif
Dylan Stockton
Kate Boggs
Richard Blake
and Simon Lipskar

Made in the USA
Middletown, DE
05 December 2023

44514752R00102